ERIN HAD TO GET AWAY FROM ALEX. SHE WAS BEING OVERWHELMED BY HIS RAW MASCULINITY.

She turned to leave, but he caught her tightly. She could only stare at him, embarrassed and a little frightened. Her eyes lingered on his lips. What would they taste like? She moistened her own in unconscious preparation and breathed a long, soft sigh. Erin felt such a sudden torrent of fire between their bodies that her legs went wobbly. Then his mouth tightly sealed her own. She could feel the hard, solid wall of his chest and then the soft touch of his fingertips stroking her silky skin. Hot, pulsing blood was flowing through her body, warming her and leading her toward a peak of exquisite torment. . . .

MARIANNA ESSEX has recently added writing romances to her longtime career as a symphony violinist. Along with writing and playing, Ms. Essex enjoys reading, studying Norwegian, and traveling with her husband. Norway and Switzerland are her favorite places and will be highlighted in future books.

Dear Reader:

The editors of Rapture Romance have only one thing to say—thank you! At a time when there are so many books to choose from, you have welcomed ours with open arms, trying new authors, coming back again and again, and writing us of your enthusiasm. Frankly, we're thrilled!

In fact, the response has been so great that we feel confident that you are ready for more stories which explore all the possibilities that exist when today's men and women fall in love. We are proud to announce that we will now be publishing six titles each month, because you've told us that four Rapture Romances simply aren't enough. Of course, we won't substitute quantity for quality! We will continue to select only the finest of sensual love stories, stories in which the passionate physical expression of love is the glorious culmination of the entire experience of falling in love.

And please keep writing to us! We love to hear from our readers, and we take your comments and opinions seriously. If you have a few minutes, we would appreciate your filling out the questionnaire at the back of this book, or feel free to write us at the address below. Some of our readers have asked how they can write to their favorite authors, and we applaud their thoughtfulness. Writers need to hear from their fans, and while we cannot give out addresses, we are more than happy to forward any mail.

Happy reading!

Robin Grunder

Rapture Romance
1633 Broadway
New York, NY 10019

TORRENT OF LOVE

by
Marianna Essex

RAPTURE ROMANCE
NEW AMERICAN LIBRARY
TIMES MIRROR

PUBLISHER'S NOTE

This novel is a work of fiction. Names, characters, places, and incidents either are the product of the author's imagination or are used fictitiously, and any resemblance to actual persons, living or dead, events, or locales is entirely coincidental.

NAL BOOKS ARE AVAILABLE AT QUANTITY DISCOUNTS
WHEN USED TO PROMOTE PRODUCTS OR SERVICES.
FOR INFORMATION PLEASE WRITE TO PREMIUM MARKETING DIVISION,
THE NEW AMERICAN LIBRARY, INC., 1633 BROADWAY,
NEW YORK, NEW YORK 10019.

Copyright © 1983 by Marianna Essex

SIGNET, SIGNET CLASSIC, MENTOR, PLUME, MERIDIAN AND NAL BOOKS
are published by The New American Library, Inc.,
1633 Broadway, New York, New York 10019

First Printing, December, 1983

1 2 3 4 5 6 7 8 9

PRINTED IN THE UNITED STATES OF AMERICA

To my family and to Ginny,
who gave and gave

Chapter One

ণ্ড

"Hold it right there, lady."

Erin Kelly turned and caught her breath at the sight of the man striding so rapidly toward her. He was big and he was boiling mad. His long legs and heavy boots weren't bothered by the mud, and he didn't seem to care that the wind was blowing his worn leather jacket open. Snowflakes clung to his red flannel shirt and were plastered to his red hard hat and long black eyelashes.

"If you've damaged my grader, lady, I'll wring that pretty little neck of yours."

"Just try it, mister. If you're so all-fired concerned about it, you should have caution signs back there. I could have been killed because of your"—she ran out of breath and had to gasp—"your negligence, and all you talk about is your stupid grader."

Only by expert manuevering had she averted a serious collision moments ago. Her Saab had spun briefly out of control in an unexpected slather of mud and clay, finally coming to a noisy, abrupt stop against a piece of road machinery. And, as if that weren't enough, the two vehicles now seemed to be locked together.

Still trembling from her close call, Erin had begun to pick her way through the mud and the puddles, jumping from one hummock of grass to another wherever possible. She had just taken one awkward leap, high heels, purse and winter coat impeding her considerably, when the sharp male voice had made her freeze. Now the man was looming over her, breathing hard and shaking his head in complete disgust.

"*Hell.*" He spat out the word and then moved to the two vehicles to assess the damage.

She finally remembered to dash away the tears on her face, tears that had nothing to do with the collision. In an uncharacteristic bout of self-pity, Erin had been weeping because she had dwelt too long and too unwisely on her ex-husband.

Now, however, Carlton Kelly was easily forgotten in the wake of this new development. Instead of tears she felt a hot wave of anger brightening her cheeks and affecting her breathing. When her next words popped out, she was gasping.

"This is absolutely unbelievable, having the road filled with all this . . . this *junk* without any warning." Her eyes darted over the yellow hulks of roadmaking and construction equipment sitting about. "It's a death trap for anyone coming around that bend in a snowstorm."

When he made no comment, Erin dabbed at her damp eyes once more, blew her nose, glared at his broad back, and fumed.

She was going to be late for her nine A.M. architectural consultation in Saxonburg, and her recently cleaned camel's-hair coat and gleaming brown pumps were mud-spattered all because of some idiot's negligence. It made her want to file charges.

She watched, blue-green eyes opened wide and heart racing, as the man rose, grim-faced and silent, and moved to the other side of her car. She could see that Mighty Mouse was tightly hooked to his miserable grader. The bumper was caught on a protuberance so that her little grimy gray bullet of a car was all askew, its right rear wheel several inches off the ground.

"I really must find a telephone," she called to him, but was met with stony silence. "*Sir.*" Erin was close to exploding. "Is there a house or gas station nearby?"

"There's a phone up in the office," came the curt reply.

She bit her lip in frustration and peered uphill through the flying snow. Lordy, wasn't that the place where those wonderful old woods used to be? The woods where she and her sister, Deirdre, used to picnic . . .

Erin blinked her eyes against the big, soft flakes brushing her face and eyelashes. It *was* the same place, the very spot! But what was that appalling sprawl there now? A shopping mall—a half-built nightmare of stone and brick and false facades.

She was thinking what an architectural abomination it was when the man finally finished his inspection and walked slowly toward her.

"Did I hear you mention negligence?" His voice was quiet.

"I certainly *did*." She stared him right in the eye, though it frightened her to do so. "No caution signs or—"

"Lady," he interrupted, making a harsh sound that Erin suspected was a laugh, "there are three caution signs back there—all spaced at the proper intervals—the largest and closest of which is right before that bend you just came barreling around at fifty miles an hour. Talk about *negligence*." The black eyes suddenly narrowed in suspicion. "Are you drunk?"

Erin's mouth dropped open and for a moment she thought he meant to smell her breath. "Drunk? I'm certainly not drunk. And it *couldn't* have been fifty." Her fingers tingled. How lovely it would be to slap his handsome, arrogant face. "It seems your signs are too tiny to be seen by anyone with normal eyesight in a blizzard like this one.''

"*Hell*." His hand suddenly closed around her upper arm, hurting her. Perhaps it wasn't intentional, but she could nevertheless feel the terrible strength in each steely finger, even through her winter coat. Erin winced in pain.

"I'm sorry . . ." He released her immediately. "I didn't mean to hurt you, but, damn it, you're going to take a look at my tiny sign." His mouth was grim.

"Why don't I just take your word that you have a sign?" She couldn't hide her exasperation. She only wanted to get on with her business and find a telephone. She positively refused to use his.

When she saw his black eyes curiously examining her face, she lifted her chin defiantly. Heavens, maybe she *did* look drunk. Her auburn curls were tousled and sprinkled with snow, her lipstick was chewed off, her mascara had probably streaked, and her eyes and nose were probably an unlovely red from her wretched bout of weeping over Carl Kelly, the rat!

Erin's features had often been described as elfin; she had a small, rounded chin, high cheekbones, and a pert nose dusted with freckles, but she doubted she looked elfin at the moment. More like the wicked witch of the west.

She was pondering her next move—getting away from him to find a telephone—when he blinked at her long, slim legs and sighed. The next thing she knew, Erin was grasped around her waist and flung over his shoulder, his right arm firmly clasping her legs the way he would handle a sack of potatoes or a bag of sand.

"You—you *clod*," she cried. The ground seemed far away, and the blood rushed so rapidly to her head that she was instantly dizzy. She squeezed her eyes shut and felt her throat close in fear. What did he mean to do with her? Erin gasped as his hands took a new grasp on her nylon-clad thighs, but it seemed impersonal; he was merely getting a firmer hold on them.

"You big oaf. Put me *down*." The worst thing in the world, she knew, was to act like an intimidated, frightened female. "*Beast*." She pounded his back with her free hand, but it was like beating a stone wall. She succeeded only in hurting herself. Not until he was good and ready did he put her down—right in front of a very large, bright-yellow sign with big black lettering: CAUTION—CONSTRUCTION AHEAD. 20 MPH.

He tilted back his hard hat and a wicked grin spread over his face. "Well?"

"I . . . I'm sorry! I didn't see it—I really didn't." Erin's cheeks were burning and she was shaken that her memories of Carl Kelly still had such an effect on her that she could miss a sign as huge as this one. It was mortifying. In eleven years of driving, she had never run afoul of the law, not even with a parking violation, and now to do *this* stupid thing. And because of this insufferable man's attitude, she couldn't even behave normally, couldn't offer him a sincere apology or even give an explanation of sorts.

"You didn't see it?" His black eyes seemed to spark with anger. When she tightened her lips to suppress an anguished rejoinder, he said, "Lady, if you didn't see that, you're a menace. You shouldn't even be on the road. Come on. I'm taking you back to your car." Erin could tell he was disgusted.

"No, thank you, I can manage on my own." But she had spoken too quickly. Looking at the morass before her, Erin instantly regretted her words.

He folded his arms across his chest and eyed her impatiently. "You know you won't dirty your feet, so let's get this over with. What will it be? The fireman's carry—over my shoulder—or in my arms?"

Heavens. How could she decide with a choice like that? Erin vowed that from now on, her construction boots would always be kept in the Saab's trunk.

"Since I don't have all day," he said, "we'll do it this way." Suddenly she was in his arms, as if she were as light as one of the snowflakes that were flying about them so wildly.

His chest was broad and hard beneath the red plaid shirt, and it was rather pleasant, she decided grudgingly, being held against this man so tightly. It had been a long time. But his attention was not on her at all, and she was just as glad.

". . . and it's a damned fine car," he was saying with irritation. "Much too fine to be mistreated. The tread's nearly gone on the rear tires, and there are rust spots all over."

The nerve of him. Erin knew he didn't expect an answer, and she didn't offer one. She would never tell this dark, angry stranger she didn't give a hoot if Mighty Mouse lived or died. The Saab had been a peace offering from her ex-husband after one of his many acts of abusing her trust.

She averted her face from his. They were barely inches apart and his breath, a steamy vapor in the cold, snowy air, was clean and warm, reminding her vaguely of bacon and eggs and coffee.

She stole a shy, sidelong glance through lowered lashes at his mouth. It was generous, with a nice, well-defined shape, cleanly cut. There was a raspy-looking dark shadow staining his jaw, several days' growth of beard, which matched his straight black eyebrows and the blue-black hair gleaming beneath his hard hat. God, he was attractive . . .

". . . and the muffler looks like it's about shot," he was going on. "Damn it, why do you have a good car if you're not going to take care of it?"

"It's hardly your affair," she gasped.

He deposited her none too gently on a dry spot on the road, then walked over to the connected vehicles and squatted once more.

Her eyes went unwillingly to the hard thighs beneath his jeans, then to his brown hands, which were moving carefully over car and grader. Tenderly, she decided, as though he were caressing a woman.

She stifled that thought immediately and, on impulse, called to him "You might tell your boss he needs a new architect for his next project, Mister. The woods that used to be here were the prettiest scenery for miles around. He might have left at least some of the trees standing."

It was the only way she could repay him for his rudeness, and she felt a childish gratification as she realized she'd hit her mark.

He shot her a black glance. "It seems you don't know much about construction, lady. Leaving pretty trees here and there puts the cost out of sight."

"Not if it's planned right. I know a little about construction costs—I happen to be an architect. Projects like this one make me see red. That awful mixture of styles, and all those unrelated ideas—those loose, dangling ends. Heavens! This area could have been *glorified*, not exploited."

"Well, well." His black eyes glittered with an odd light. "And which eminent authority are you?"

"I'm Erin Kelly of Earth Architecture."

He stood up, having finally decided what had to be done, and did it. He grasped Mighty Mouse's rear end and emitted a loud grunt as he lifted it off the grader. He then gave the grader another careful inspection and started toward her. He was limping severely and Erin gasped in surprise. What in the world had happened?

"My name is Alex Butler," he said gruffly, "and I'd like to hear just what it is that you, in your infinite wisdom, would do to improve what's already here."

"You're *limping*. You've hurt yourself lifting my car." Her eyes widened with concern and compassion.

"Don't bother yourself about me." The tone was brusque. "Just answer the question."

She brushed impatiently at the thick snowflakes tickling her face and clinging to her eyelashes. *Damn*. Why had she allowed her foolish tongue such freedom? She had just insulted a complete stranger and now he was towering over her and demanding an explanation.

Her troubled eyes took in the tasteless sprawl on the hill. Most people, she knew, wouldn't see anything wrong with it, but she had been taught that a structure must embody the characteristics of the region in which it is built. It must have poise and natural elegance and serenity. She believed that with her whole heart, but how could she tactfully tell him how she felt: This . . . this *thing* was so unmemorable, so unappealing. And she was so inept at lying. She caught her lower lip between her teeth.

"That bad, eh?"

Erin made herself face him. "It's only one person's opinion, Mr. Butler."

"And that opinion is?"

"I think I'd be tempted to"—she had to clear her throat—"abandon it and start over."

She held her breath and waited for an explosion of ridicule and sarcasm. Cruel, cutting words. Erin was surprised when an impassive shadow touched his face and a far-off, dreamy look entered his eyes that she couldn't quite understand. It had a quieting effect on her, and from that inner quiet, she realized just how unprofessionally she had behaved. She had gotten her revenge in an almost childish way and she instantly regretted it.

"I'm sorry. I really shouldn't have said anything bad about the mall. I'm certain most people will like it." Her hand went uncertainly to her hair and dislodged some of the snow, which immediately tumbled down the back of her neck. Erin gave a small shudder. "Anyway, thank you for freeing my car. I really wouldn't want your boss to know what I said—it was uncalled for. I wouldn't want to hurt his feelings."

"You flatter yourself." The dreaminess had left his eyes and she shivered again, not from the cold but from his expression. It was as though molten steel were glowing in his eyes. "My feelings aren't hurt in the least," he said. "Butler Builders is fairly successful, despite its flawed architecture."

Alex Butler—Butler Builders.

"My goodness, I . . ."

He had taken her arm and was gently but firmly leading her to her car, avoiding the worst of the mud.

"I really . . . I'm so . . ." Erin's wits were so completely scattered she thought it best not to talk at all.

He opened the door and politely handed her in. "Promise me that you'll watch the posted speed limits now. At least until you get the hell out of here." The slamming of the car door seemed a final, angry punctuation to his words.

Her hand trembled as she turned the key in the ignition, then fed gas to the Saab. It bumped slowly over the icy ruts and splashed through deep water.

Erin peered into her rearview mirror just in time to catch a final glimpse of Alex Butler. He was limping, obviously in pain, slowly heading up the hill towards his ugly mall. Her heart gave a little twist, as though a hand had reached in and squeezed it.

Lordy, she *would* have to act like a bulldozer, with her brains in low gear and her mouth in high. All of a sudden it became as plain as day why the man had behaved that way; he was hurting and grieving, and that strange, dreamy look in his eyes—the look she couldn't pinpoint—was sadness.

Erin sighed as she shifted smoothly through the gears. What a way to start her morning, and now she'd somehow have to make up for lost time. At least the snow wasn't piling up. She took a quick, distressed look at herself in the rearview mirror. She really would have to repair her makeup, modest though it was, before the Saxonburg meeting.

Lord, she felt dismal. She was still jittery and upset over her tangle with Alex Butler. To think she had been allowing herself to wallow in five minutes of delicious self-pity—*five minutes*—when she turned that bend and might have killed herself.

The self-pity had come because she was passing so many farmhouses, their lights warm and inviting against the darkening sky. Prim Pennsylvania farmhouses with families inside eating breakfast, planning the day over coffee, and getting the children off to school. And here she was, Erin Corcoran Kelly, twenty-seven, alone, childless, and with a failed marriage behind her.

That's it, she told herself, taking a determined breath. Enough's enough. She had a good life now—a new life. Her own architectural firm in the Shadyside section of Pittsburgh was growing, she was renting a charming old farmhouse in Glenshaw, and last year she had won a competition in Mexico; her name was finally becoming known in architectural circles.

And she was near Deirdre again—that was important. It was her sister, in fact, who had coaxed Erin back to their "homeland." They had different tastes and life-styles, but the sisters' love for each other was deep and they laughed together over the silliest things. It was wonderful to be near her again and have her helping in the office. Deirdre was her only family now . . .

It was shortly before noon when Erin, her consultation over, finally got back to Shadyside. As she crept through the busy streets, she decided that the morning had been successful enough to be celebrated despite its unfortunate beginning. Even the weather had turned festive, with blue skies and sunshine, and felt almost like a spring day.

When a parking spot opened up in front of the deli, it seemed a happy bit of luck. Fifteen minutes later, she entered her office carrying a full brown paper bag.

"Deirdre, love, plug in the coffeepot."

"Hello. What's happening?" Deirdre was just replacing the telephone receiver.

"The Saxonburg people really liked the drawings and specs." Erin's cheeks were pink with excitement. "And a woman was there who's on the building committee for that new hospital wing in Natrona Heights. I'm to go up next week and talk with them."

Erin held up the bag like a banner. "We're *celebrating*." She rapidly set out the feast on one end of her desk: corned beef on rye, kosher pickles, and cheesecake. The two small rooms that constituted Earth Architecture were immediately filled with tantalizing odors.

"How divine." Deirdre's eyes, so much like her younger sister's, widened.

Erin deposited her coat on the clothes tree in the corner and pulled up a chair to dig in. She was chewing away while Deirdre was still cutting her sandwich into four dainty pieces after spreading a napkin across her lap.

Erin knew she resembled Deirdre physically, but no one would ever mistake one sister for the other. Deirdre's auburn hair was chic: shoulder length, straight, and either caught back under a simple tortoiseshell hairband or worn in a sleek chignon.

Her skin bore a carefully preserved tan, and her jewelry—sumptuous gold chains and bracelets—clinked when she moved. And her clothes. Sighing, Erin looked over her corned beef at Deirdre's blue silk shirt and beige cashmere skirt. Positively gorgeous.

But despite her appearance, Clyde Cunningham hadn't left Deirdre a wealthy Shadyside widow when he'd died of a heart attack two years ago. Comfortable, yes; wealthy, no. And she was lonely. Luckily for Erin, Deirdre was thrilled to be helping her younger sister and worked as her secretary/receptionist and public relations person for only a small salary.

"We had a few calls while you were out," Deirdre said casually. "Someone from Soho asking if you were interested in urban renovation." Erin shook her head and wrinkled her nose. "And someone from the East End wondering if you did theater design."

"It might be fun." She had done mostly private homes, but her triumph in Mexico had been a concert hall.

"And"—Deirdre paused for dramatic effect— "Nicholas van Rijn called."

"*Nicholas van Rijn.*" Erin put down her sandwich and, still chewing, stared at her beaming sister. "Called from where? And why?"

"From Oakland, where he's been living for the past year. Imagine, all this time he's lived just five minutes from here. He wants to talk with you. It seems he's thinking of building a summer home."

Nicholas van Rijn . . . Erin hadn't seen him for—she counted back—eleven years. The very name recalled all sorts of memories: her parents' big, comfortable home in Fox Chapel, the swimming pool in the backyard, lots of parties, and a way of life she would probably never know again. Her father, Quintus Corcoran, had been a wealthy man until the unexpected loss of his business.

Van had been a business associate of her father's but much younger. A tall, blond Dutchman, newly arrived from Holland, he had a fascinating accent and piercing blue eyes. Erin had loved him, secretly and hopelessly, from the moment she laid eyes on him. He was divorced, which had made him even more forbidden to a sixteen-year-old, and not even Deirdre had known about the infatuation that tied Erin's tongue when she was near him and kept her in tears for weeks when he had eventually married again and moved away.

"He'll call again at two." Deirdre took a dainty bite of her sandwich.

Erin munched thoughtfully on a pickle. "What did he sound like?"

"Oh, European still. Elegant. And very polite. The same, in other words." Deirdre poured the coffee. "Oh, Erin, what a plum if he commissions you. Nicholas is wealthy—he's in the Allegheny Tower now—and I'm sure he knows everyone who's anyone. I'm *so* excited. Oh, my clever baby sister!" She grabbed Erin's hand and squeezed it.

Erin grinned and returned the squeeze.

"Don't get too excited just yet," she cautioned, but it was wonderful seeing Deirdre so happy over her success. Touching, in fact.

As interesting as Deirdre's news was, Erin didn't want to talk about Nicholas van Rijn just then. All morning long her irritating yet intriguing encounter with Alex Butler had tormented her. She'd been dying to tell Deirdre about it, because the more she thought about it, the more she felt that she knew the name.

"Does the name Alex Butler mean anything to you?" Erin asked suddenly.

"King Butler's son? Erin! Don't you remember the Butlers? They belonged to our country club. Alex was positively the most divine thing there, but all he cared about was automobile transmissions, downhill skiing, and flying. It was a crime he was so late getting interested in girls."

The country club. For some childish reason Erin had hated the place and had gone only when forced to. She certainly didn't remember Alex Butler.

"We were both seventeen," Deirdre went on, "and I used every trick in the book to get him to notice me."

Her sister's book of tricks, Erin happened to know, had been encyclopedic. Alex Butler *must* have been blind. She drank some coffee and raked her memory. If Deirdre was seventeen, she had been ten. A very pesky and headstrong ten.

"Darling," Deirdre cried suddenly, "he drove that cute little car you were so wild about. A little ed MG convertible. You were all eyes."

It was like one of those crazy cartoons in which the light bulb goes on. Now that Erin had a point of reference, it was there—a nebulous, undefined memory of a tall, dark boy in a wonderful little toy of a car. She had coveted *it*, not the boy.

Relieved at having remembered, she rose, walked about the room and kneaded a tight little muscle in the back of her neck. So long ago . . . Her eyes moved fondly over Quintus Corcoran's old rolltop desk and chair and the Oriental rug from her mother's sewing room. Her memories of those precious things and of the red car were of the same vintage—memories that made her feel mellow just thinking of them.

"Now do you remember?"

"Mmm, I remember," she answered dreamily.

"And I remember what a funny little thing you were. Always wanting to play tennis with me and asking me to

take you to that awful stable on Deerfield Road to ride
Western when we belonged to a perfectly marvelous riding
club where you would have been taught to ride properly—
English. Ah, well.'' Deirdre patted Erin's hand and
showered her with a smile of pure admiration. ''You
turned out beautifully in spite of all your little quirks.
But, darling, do go on about Alex Butler. Why did you ask
about him?''

''I sort of . . . ran into him today.'' She would tell Deirdre the gory details later on, but now she sat down and
took another bite of her sandwich. ''Did you know he's a
builder?''

Deirdre shook her head. ''I lost touch with all those
people after the house was sold.''

Their parents' home. Neither was in the mood for such
painful talk, and Erin was glad when Deirdre plunged on
about Alex.

''I did hear ages ago that Alex had disappointed his
family and gone into something rather tacky—for a
Butler, that is. He was supposed to carry on the family
tradition.''

''It sounds formidable. What tradition?''

''Judges and lawyers. You really don't remember anything at all?''

No. Erin didn't remember anything at all about those
clubs, or the people who belonged to them, except that
dim memory of Alex Butler in his magical car. A young boy
meant to be a judge or a lawyer.

Her sister was right; she had been a funny little thing,
embarrassed by her father's prosperity and much happier
with those friends whose parents didn't belong to country
clubs and racquet clubs and riding clubs.

''When did Alex finally notice girls?'' Erin asked.

''The summer after graduation. And with a vengeance, I
might add. Unfortunately he didn't notice *this* girl. Then

off he went to college and so did I, and then I married
Clyde . . ." She shrugged. That's life, the casual gesture
seemed to say. Then she looked thoughtful. "I seem to
recall an exotic bit of gossip about Alex. Something about
unrequited love. Now, who in the world told me that, and
when?"

The phone rang just then and it was Nicholas van Rijn,
calling at two P.M. precisely. Their conversation was brief
and when Erin hung up, Deirdre wanted to hear every
word.

"What's happening?"

"He's calling for me at six and we'll be dining at the
White Bark Country Club." Erin wiggled her eyebrows
and grinned impishly. "A business meeting, love."

"Oh, you lucky, lucky dog."

Chapter Two

As Nicholas van Rijn smiled at her over a glowing candle in the White Bark lounge, Erin decided that he was even more handsome than she remembered. His fair hair, now streaked with gray, was wonderfully distinguished, and the deep lines etched about his eyes and mouth marked him as an important person; he was now the president of a large corporation. Nicholas van Rijn, in his late forties, was a solid, impressive figure.

"My dear, it's been much too long. I want to hear everything." His accent had the same charm that had made Erin swoon with delight so long ago.

"Van, you don't know what you're saying." She laughed and sank back gratefully into the soft, velvet-upholstered chair.

It was lovely having Nicholas van Rijn take complete charge of her evening. He had brought her to this elegant place in a black, chauffeur-driven Mercedes, and now she listened as he ordered a chilled bottle of imported Bolta Chablis for them to drink before dinner.

Erin hadn't realized how edgy she was until the first few sips of wine warmed her throat and began to relax her. Between her encounter with Alex Butler and the consultation, it had been a trying day, but it was ending well.

She suddenly had the most delicious feeling, as though she had been magically transported into an old romantic movie starring Cary Grant or Charles Boyer. First the limousine and now all this elegance and lovely wine. Even her own clothing. Erin had worn one of the few stunning things she owned, a deep-green silk dress, gracefully draped to tie at her waist, cut low in the front, and slit at the side to show a discreet glimpse of her left leg above the knee. She had smoothed her hair behind her ears, glad that it was behaving for once, and added a pair of small pearl earrings to her ears.

Van's next words brought her back to the present. "Erin, I must tell you how saddened I was to hear about Quintus and Mary. First the reversal in his business, and then . . ." He shook his head gravely. "I am so sorry."

"Thank you." The numbness was long gone, but she never would get over the loss of her parents seven years ago in an earthquake in Mexico.

"Now, tell me," he said as his kindly eyes took in her bare left hand, "you are married?"

"I've been divorced for three years." She calmly sipped her Chablis.

He shrugged, almost carelessly. "Ah. I, too, have had my troubles that way. Two wives so far, and both impossible."

"How is your daughter?" Erin had seen the girl only once during Van's association with her father. The child had been ten or eleven at the time and so chic even then that Erin had felt downright dowdy in comparison.

"Cecile is smart and beautiful, naturally." Van smiled.

"She would be."

"Have you children?" he asked.

"No." She managed a smile and declared that, having married at nineteen and divorced at twenty-four, there had been little time for a child. During the marriage she had been going to college full time, doing the cooking and all the housework, and studying into the night. She hadn't minded, of course—she had thrived on it because she was in love. But had she and Carl stayed together, she would certainly have wanted a baby.

"This Carlton Kelly was a professor?" Van removed the wine bottle from the ice bucket and poured more Chablis into her glass.

"Yes, he taught architectural design when I was a freshman." And she had fallen in love with him the night she'd met him—head over heels and right off the bat. Just as she had with Van, Erin thought gloomily. She wondered if that terrible pattern would repeat itself throughout her life.

Van wanted to hear about her divorce and she told him as briefly as possible: Carl had left academia and started his own firm shortly after their marriage, and almost two years had passed before she realized he was using some of her own work, altering it and passing it off as his own. And if that weren't enough, there were his roving eyes and hands and that woman he had kept during the last year of their marriage.

Though Van was comforting, Erin didn't want to waste this lovely evening talking about Carlton Kelly and his sticky fingers!

"I'd rather not talk about it anymore if you don't mind." She lifted her glass to her lips, relishing the relaxed and carefree atmosphere between them. The Chablis warmed her, and the evening seemed to take on a magical ambience.

"Enough about me, Van. I want to hear about you." She gave him a dewy smile across the table. "I want to hear all about this summer home you're planning. What sort of house and where it will be and how you intend to use it and—"

Van laughed and held up a restraining hand. "What sort

of house will be up to you, I think. I have no feel for that sort of thing."

"Van, you're kidding me." Erin gaped at him. Most clients had too much to say and very little of it was practical.

"Not at all. I've chosen you to design it, Erin, and whatever you decide will be all right with me. The rest of your questions I will answer when my other dinner guest arrives. Ah, I believe I see him now."

Her eyes followed Van's gaze across the lounge. A very tall, very dark man had just stopped to talk with three women. He seemed familiar, and she blinked to clear her vision. It was something about the way he shrugged his shoulders and gestured broadly with his arm as he described something. Her mouth didn't quite fall open.

Oh, God. The last time she saw that gesture, he was wearing a red hard hat and pointing out a yellow caution sign to her. Now he was headed their way and Erin had to put a hand on her breast to quiet the clamor inside.

"Alex, thank you for coming." Van stood up and the two men shook hands warmly.

Alex Butler's surprised black eyes were already on Erin, and she suspected she was as red as a beet, not a flattering color for someone with auburn hair. She wasn't sure she appreciated that knowing smile on his lips.

"Erin, I want you to meet Alexander King Butler. Alex, this is Erin Kelly."

"We've . . . already met," Erin said to Van, and gave a stiff little nod in Alex's direction.

"Just this morning, in fact." Alex Butler was still smiling, as though she were a delicious pastry he was about to sample.

"Well, then," said Van, unaware that anything was amiss, "get yourself a drink, Alex, and we can go into the dining room." He consulted his watch. "Excuse me. I must first make a call."

As Van walked away Erin could sense that Alex Butler was looking at her.

"Hmmm. You look better than you did this morning," he said, taking the seat beside hers. His amused eyes dwelt on her sleek hair and lustrous earrings for a long moment before moving on to savor the rest of her.

"Thank you." She made herself smile sweetly. "You've improved considerably yourself."

When Erin realized where his gaze was resting, she casually brushed an imaginary speck from one green silk sleeve. It blocked his view of her low neckline, but only momentarily, and she suspected the sudden warmth she felt all over had gone to her cheeks in a fiery blush. She felt positively naked with him looking at her like that.

This Alex Butler, she thought resentfully, was a far cry from that sad, limping man she had seen in her rearview mirror that morning. He was dressed in a navy suit, a crisp, snowy shirt, and a striped tie. His blue-black hair was thick and glossy, and he was cleanly shaven. He was neither limping nor grieving. Far from it. He seemed fit, happy, and full of the devil. Actually, Erin decided, she liked him better when he was scowling, crabby, and sad.

He ordered his drink and when Van returned they all headed into the dining room for dinner. Erin was starving. She hadn't eaten a speck of food since the celebratory corned beef at noon.

"Well, now," said Van after they'd ordered, "let me tell you what this is all about. I have a considerable amount of land north of Pittsburgh. There are seven hundred heavily wooded acres, and there's also a lake on the property. It has a dirt access road and wiring for electricity . . ."

Erin watched Van over the candle's golden glow and listened to his words, but her mind was elsewhere. What a shock to be sitting across from Alex Butler. Why, she'd hardly recovered from that fracas with him this morning.

"I think a house could be built in that valley," Van was saying. "The site is between two bluffs and it has a fine, clear stream coming down off the hill."

Erin's eyes met Alex's just then and she could see the flames reflected from the candle in them. But wait—it was more than that. There was a hot, brief glimmer of interest before he looked back at Van and nodded. She felt a sweet twinge deep inside her body. The look hadn't been bold or out of place; it had only said that he found her very attractive.

Incredible. When Erin had gone to sleep the previous night, she hadn't even known this man. Today, they had already exchanged insults, he'd carried her in his arms—not to mention over his shoulder—and now he was sending her messages across a candlelit table. And, much to Erin's chagrin, her body was responding with a will of its own, despite her coolness toward him.

Van was still talking about his land and how valuable it was, and she felt her foot start to tap under the table. No matter how attractive Alex Butler was, Erin had no intention of collaborating with him on anything. It surprised her that Van should be trying to commit the two of them, right here and now, to build his house. But, then, perhaps that was his way—she didn't really know him.

"What do you say, my dear?" Van was regarding her with piercing blue eyes. "Will you be on my team to get a house on that land?"

No, she wanted to snap. I will not be on your "team"—not if it includes him. Erin had always insisted on selecting the contractor, and this man was building that sprawling monstrosity of a shopping mall. He hadn't left even one tree standing.

But she was in a velvet trap, being wined and dined and cosseted by a family friend, a man she had loved when she was young. Erin didn't want to offend him, nor did she want to make an enemy of Alex Butler. She had already insulted him enough for one day.

"I'd like a chance to think it over, Van." She was saved by the arrival of dinner; there seemed to be a silent agreement between the men not to discuss business while eating.

Erin was more than content to listen to their talk about the Steelers and Pittsburgh politics and the economy, joining in whenever she had a point to make. Her mind, however, was exploring her dilemma.

She knew instinctively that this dark, good-looking stranger sitting across the table would obstruct her intentions and object to anything innovative she might want to do. Erin didn't like to work that way. And yet the project was too intriguing simply to turn it down point-blank. It was an architect's dream to get a chance to design a house any way she wanted. And Deirdre had been right: Van knew people and had influence. Pleasing him would be a big career step.

"I think you'll like the site, Erin," Van said, resuming their earlier conversation as the waiter cleared the table. "It's quiet, the lake is beautiful, there are deer . . ."

He poured himself a glass of Bolta port and offered to fill her glass. She shook her head. Her thoughts were whirling as it was, and she must tread softly and keep all her wits about her.

"I'd be afraid to do it, Van. What if I came up with something that was all 'me'? You'd probably be too polite to complain, and end up with something you hated." Actually, she thought no such thing, but, plain and simple, she was floundering about what to say or do.

Van laughed. "Ah, I am *never* so polite."

She shot a wide-eyed glance at Alex Butler, a look of appeal. Surely he wouldn't want to work with her.

Pinpoint flames glittered in the eyes that looked back at her. He was waiting and he was curious. Erin felt the same fluttering of her heart that she had felt that morning when he'd seemed so vulnerable.

No. She pulled herself up with a jolt. Not *this* man, Erin Kelly. It was an established fact she could fall like a ton of bricks and just as fast. No, no, no—not *this* one. But she could barely take her eyes off him. There was a terrible fascination in the way the slanting shadows from the candle emphasized the strong planes of his face and highlighted his shiny black hair.

"Van, I . . . I will have some wine, please. Just half a glass." She clutched the fragile stem of the goblet so tightly that Van noticed.

"My dear, I'm sorry. I have upset you and I didn't mean to." He gave her a fatherly pat on the arm. "I won't insist on an answer tonight. Relax now and we will—"

Alex's deep voice interrupted him. "I think Miss Kelly and I agree on—"

"It's Mrs. Kelly, Alex," Van said.

"It's *Ms.* Kelly," Erin interjected, hating the thin, high squeak her vocal cords had produced.

Alex's black eyes looked at her across the table. "As I was saying, Van, *Ms.* Kelly and I agree on this subject. We have different ideas about architecture, and we don't have the . . . the necessary rapport to work together."

"*Rapport?*" There was steel in Van's eyes for the first time. "What has rapport to do with building a house, my friends?"

Erin gave Alex a grateful smile. "Van, he's right. I'm afraid the only thing Mr. Butler and I may have in common is a quick temper. And we'd be thrown together constantly if we agreed to work on your house."

When Van gave her a look of disbelief, she continued. "I'd be your go-between for everything from the bonds and insurance to the final billing. We can't be snapping each other's heads off all that while."

"I see. Well, I am disappointed, but perhaps I have taken you both too much by surprise. This has been a sudden decision, even for me. Take several days to think it over, and, as a personal favor, please look at the property before you say no."

When she and Alex both agreed, Van reached into an inner coat pocket and drew forth two small, folded sheets of paper. The directions to his property and Laurel Lake.

Erin tucked hers into her purse. She was grateful that, for such an uncomfortable situation, it had had a fairly happy conclusion. She also had to admit that it had been downright decent of Alex Butler to do what he had— recognize her silent plea for help and come to the rescue. She sighed. A rescue for the second time this day. The man couldn't be all that bad.

It was during dessert that she caught him staring at her. Self-consciously she touched her hair; it would accept confinement only for a limited amount of time and sure enough, that time was up. Now it curled softly, tousled and as bright as autumn leaves against her white skin. No doubt her lipstick was all gone, too, just as it had been that morning. She flicked a pink tongue over her soft lips. Yes. It was gone.

Erin felt as if she had turned back into a frog and it wasn't even midnight yet. Alex Butler was still staring, wondering, no doubt, how she had managed the metamorphosis. She blinked, confused by his scrutiny.

Van took that moment to make another phone call and she froze as Alex leaned toward her. "Did you know, Ms. Kelly"—his voice was very low—"that I was torn this morning between throttling you and kissing you?"

"I . . . I didn't know." Erin was shocked. She had only an unpleasant and a tangible impression of his anger and disgust. That and the sadness.

"It's true." He nodded matter-of-factly as his eyes traveled over the silky green dress that made her skin look so soft and white. "And all that talk about rapport got me to thinking. You and I would have plenty of rapport if we just gave it a try."

If Erin's heart beat any faster, she felt sure it would burst.

"What do you say, Ms. Kelly?" His voice sounded husky and intimate.

"I . . . think not, Mr. Butler." Without a doubt, he was the first real threat to her since her divorce. Erin refused to tangle with him and take the chance of being hurt again.

"I can feel it already, can't you?"

That was just the trouble. She *could* feel it. His dark, sexy attractiveness was making her squirm inside and she could vividly remember being squeezed against his chest, weightless and helpless. She took in a long breath, gathering her determination, but before she could open her mouth his hands had covered hers. They were warm and gentle, but Erin could feel the underlying strength in the man.

"I think you and I would be dynamite together," he went on, coaxing, "but not on a building site."

"Well, then, I can only be thankful that's not likely to happen."

She blinked as the words popped out. That wasn't what she'd meant to say at all. At least not in such a snippy, prissy way. She could have said the same thing kindly, but for some reason her wits and her tongue didn't behave normally when he was so close to her. Alex seemed to bring out the worst in her. She struggled to free herself from his dark charisma.

"My loss," he said politely, and removed his hands from hers.

"Heavens, I put that very badly. I'm sorry."

He shrugged but his smile was gone. Van was coming back with her coat over his arm and she had only seconds to whisper, "I *am* sorry, and it's—it's me! Not you."

Good-byes were said and then she was ensconced in the Mercedes, with Van's solid form beside her as they were whisked off to Glenshaw.

"You're quiet, Erin."

"Oh, I was just thinking about the wonderful evening."

Van gave a pleased chuckle and talked on about one thing and another. Erin murmured an occasional comment, and he seemed satisfied to expound uninterrupted. It was just as well. All she could think about was the polite mask on Alex Butler's face as the Mercedes had pulled away.

She'd done it again—insulted him with her sassy words before she could curb her tongue. Erin sighed into the turned-up collar of her black wool greatcoat. If he were the one who was insulted and rejected, why did she feel so crushed?

The next morning, Erin was already busy over the drafting board when Deirdre arrived at the office bearing bagels and cream cheese.

"Hello, love." She looked up. "Umm. *Food.*" Erin hadn't been able to eat a bite before leaving home. Nerves, she supposed.

Her night had been bad. When she'd finally slept, it was uneasily; she'd twisted the sheets with her thrashing, and had had terrible dreams. In them, Alex Butler kept insisting that all the trees on Van's lot had to come down and that her design was ugly and damned impractical.

But the dreams, as miserable as they had been, were infinitely preferable to the way she had lain awake in the dark with her heart racing and her eyes wide open. He wanted to kiss her, he'd said, and Erin had imagined that kiss in a hundred different ways, each more exciting than the last.

"I want to hear all," Deirdre commanded, interrupting Erin's daydreams. "From beginning to end." She laid out the bagels and cheese. "You know, I think we need a little fridge here—a tiny one. You're always starving, and this place will be hot in the summer. Nothing will keep. We'll check the Goodwill. Now," she said in the same breath, "what happened last night?"

It was only then that Deirdre got a good look at her younger sister. "Darling, what's *wrong*? You've got black circles under your eyes, and your hair is all askew. What in the world. . . ?"

Erin sighed. She couldn't keep anything from Deirdre. "For a start, I didn't have breakfast." She broke a bagel in half and listlessly dabbed some cream cheese on it.

"*You* didn't eat? Are you ill?"

Erin flung her an anguished look. Actually, she did feel rather sick.

"Was it something that happened last night?" Deirdre's eyes were suddenly flashing like those of a mother lion protecting her threatened cub. "Did that Nicholas van Rijn give you a hard time? That old *goat*."

Erin burst into laughter. "Old goat" hardly described Nicholas van Rijn. "Oh, Deirdre, you're wonderful. Do you know how much I love you?" She leaped up and flung her arms around her sister's slender, elegantly clad shoulders.

"Actually, I had a great time last night and Van was a perfect gentleman. I was driven to and from the club in a black Mercedes about as long as this block, and since

White Bark is the plushest thing around, the food was superb. Van definitely wants me to do his house. The location sounds wonderful and I'm excited about it—''

"So what's wrong?" Deirdre drummed her fingers on the tabletop. "Something is wrong. You're much too bright."

Erin put down the bagel, still unable to eat. "The Corcoran genes ride again," she said gloomily.

Deirdre had been about to sip her coffee, but she stopped short and watched as Erin ran her fingers through her hair, tousling it further, and then buried her face in her hands.

"Darling, you're positively distraught. What in the world do you mean, 'the Corcoran genes ride again'?"

"Genes. They're a curse, that's what they are.'' Her voice was muffled. "But you obviously aren't afflicted like the rest of us. Granddad Corcoran fell in love at first sight—remember Grandma telling us that funny story? Then Daddy fell for Mother right off the bat." They were both silent at the nostalgic thought. "And it was the same with Aunt Pat and Aunt Maggie—all Corcorans. Then I fell for Carl the first time I saw him, and you never knew it but I fell for Van when I was sixteen. I was wild about him."

"You? Why, you were only a baby," Deirdre said. "I was the one who really fell for him."

"You *didn't.*" Erin looked up at her, incredulous.

"I did. And I cried for days when he married that snippy Texan. I was away at college, you know. But oh, Erin, listen to this—I'm smitten again. Just hearing his deep voice on the phone leaves me positively weak."

"Deirdre."

"Erin, is *that* what's wrong? Oh, darling. You've fallen for Nicholas all over again."

"No." Erin was half laughing, half crying. "You're not

going to believe this, but I have a crush on your old heart throb, Alex Butler.''

"Alex? Where does he fit into all this?"

"He was Van's other guest last night. Van wants him to build the house."

Erin poured out the whole story then, from her close call in the car, and how furious they both were, to how ugly Alex's mall was and how the once-beautiful woods where they used to picnic had been totally obliterated.

Deirdre listened, blinking her blue eyes and zeroing in on one thing. "Threw you over his shoulder? Darling, how positively *gauche*. Whatever was he thinking of?"

Erin shrugged. What had happened that morning no longer mattered, she said. Now she had a larger problem to deal with: Alex Butler attracted her more than any other man she had met recently. But if she had learned anything from her marriage to Carlton Kelly, it was that a man had to have principles. Principles and values.

"Principles? Just to go out with for a good time and date occasionally? I think you're making too much of it. And I don't quite see why, if you like him, you don't want to work with him. You wouldn't be doing a mall with him, darling. Just a little house. It would be such fun for you—a little romance with Alex . . ."

"It's not that simple." It was clear Deirdre didn't understand. Erin was afraid, wretchedly afraid of being hurt again. Right now it was nothing but attraction, she told herself, and that's all she intended it to be. She wouldn't encourage it.

"Darling, you said there were sparks flying between you. Why fight it?"

Erin shook her head glumly and changed her tack. She and Deirdre would never agree on this subject. "I just don't care for big-time builders."

"But surely Alex isn't one of those appalling people. He was so sweet."

"He's on his way." Erin sniffed. "As of this hour, he stands for everything I'm against."

"Is he corrupt? Poor King and Sandra."

"I was speaking about architecture," Erin said.

"Darling, people *do* have to live, you know. They need to have a place to buy things and most people don't care what a mall looks like."

"But it's just as easy to build something simple and elegant as it is to build something hideous." Erin was getting up a good head of steam. Actually, it was a relief to think of Alex's ugly mall, for then she wasn't thinking of his black glittering eyes.

"Erin," said Deirdre, "calm down. Eat the rest of your bagel and when Nicholas calls, just tell him you want another builder."

"Don't think I *won't*." She had already determined to do that very thing; she'd just needed Deirdre's push. Suddenly heartened, Erin finished eating her first bagel, then slathered a generous amount of cream cheese on a second one. Her appetite was restored.

Chapter Three

❧

When the telephone rang, Deirdre answered. It was Van. After a brief chat with him she handed Erin the phone, beaming as though it were Christmas morning. "Oh, I just adore his accent," she whispered.

"Good morning, Van." Erin gave her sister an impish smile; perhaps she could somehow manage to get the two of them together.

"Good morning, my dear. I enjoyed last night. I hope you did, too."

"It was a lovely evening. Thanks again."

"I called to say I'm free this afternoon. Could you take a spin up to Laurel Lake with me? It's such a fine day for a drive."

"Van, I'd love to but I have an appointment this afternoon. I'm so sorry."

"Well, then, another time, perhaps. I'm leaving for California this evening and I won't return until next week."

She blew out a soft little sigh. She might as well come right out with it.

"Van . . ."

"My dear?"

Erin was nervously drawing little black squiggles on the pad beside the telephone. "If I should do your house, I'm

. . . well, I'm used to picking my own builder. Roberto Strata is very competent.''

"Indeed . . ." There was a considerable pause. "I'm sorry, my dear, but it isn't for—" Van stopped in mid-sentence and laughed. "Let's save this discussion until you say you'll do my house." His tone of voice said that was final.

That Friday was a glorious day, and since Deirdre was willing to mind the office, Erin gassed up the Saab and headed north. She followed the little map Van had given her and took Route 8 onto the turnpike, then north on I-79. When she neared Moraine State Park, Erin knew she was somewhere in the vicinity. She wondered, in fact, if that vast stand of pines far off to her right might be part of Van's property.

It was. She soon found the narrow, muddy road that was wide enough for only one car. She crept slowly to the top of the bluff Van had mentioned, then got out and stood looking down into a steep ravine. It seemed like a jungle at first, filled with spiky bushes and ferns and a swiftly running creek, Otter Run. Why, it *was* a wilderness. Surely Van didn't really think a house could be built here?

Erin half slid, half fell down the steep, muddy path, glad that she had worn old, comfortable clothing that could take the mud and the brambles. Her heavy jeans were tucked into tall rubber boots, and a green sweat shirt and an old blue survival jacket warded off the crisp air.

After the first, steep descent into the ravine, there were several broad, level terraces that were covered with pines, maples, and rhododendrons. There were massive boulders everywhere; huge slabs that had been left there eons ago by a receding glacier. The creek bed itself was filled with jagged pieces of rock standing every which way with water tumbling about them.

Van had been right, she thought. It was a place that would be lovely in all seasons because of the profusion of evergreens and the excitement of the rushing water and the lake. She wandered about, enchanted, and lost all track of time as she viewed the valley from many different angles.

Erin especially liked the spot where a great monolith had been tossed close to the falls—a full, white, eight-foot-high cascade of clear spring water.

She sat down on a fallen log as a little current of excitement began to hum through her body. That very spot, she knew instinctively, was the place for the house. She wasn't sure yet just how she would work it, but that boulder—that symbol of stability in a haphazard world—had to be included.

There was that sketch she had done her junior year in college: a glass and redwood house with a large terrace. When Erin visualized it there, she liked the picture it made. All that glass would bring the glorious beauty inside, and with a terrace, one could enjoy the wilderness and the wild water from a secure haven.

Her heart skipped a beat. Carl had seen the sketch, naturally, for she had been proud of it and had shown it to him. She was suddenly sobered. Maybe her precious house was already standing out there somewhere . . .

She would never know just how many of her ideas had gone out of his office with her former husband's name on them. Not that they had been anything special in those days, but still . . . Erin shook her head; she didn't want to start thinking about that.

The faint, buzzing noise she had been hearing for some time was suddenly a loud clatter overhead and she leaped up. A helicopter was beating its way up the valley and finally disappeared over the edge of the bluff. It was a yellow helicopter with a big blue BB on its side. It took only an instant for Erin to realize that the BB stood for Butler Builders, and that it was most likely Alex Butler himself coming to look at the site. He was keeping his promise to Nicholas van Rijn, just as she was. Oh, God.

She would have gladly fled undetected, but Mighty Mouse was at the top of the cliff and so was the chopper. Please, she prayed, don't let him be alone. Then she rationalized that of course he wouldn't be alone; he would have a pilot with him.

Erin was wrong. Alex *was* alone, or else the pilot had stayed with the helicopter. She saw his tall, hatless form moving easily down the steep path long before he saw her. She was tempted just to watch him, but he knew she was there somewhere and she finally called to him just to get it over with.

"Hello," he called back without any great show of enthusiasm.

He was taller than she remembered, and he was chillingly businesslike.

"Have you looked it over yet?" Alex asked.

She nodded. "Yes. I think Van is right. I like it."

His eyes narrowed as he looked around and then back at her. Erin took an involuntary step backward. She was still wondering, damn it, what his mouth would feel and taste like.

"Is something the matter?" he asked, so politely she wanted to kick him. When she shook her head, he said, "If you'll excuse me, then, I'll go ahead and look around."

The impassive mask he had put on that evening still tightened his features and she silently scolded herself. Don't complain, Erin Kelly. You've brought this all on yourself and he's giving you exactly what you wanted.

Aloud she said brightly, "I was just about to take some notes." She settled herself on the log again, got out her pad, flipped it open and started scribbling copiously—

questions for Van, questions for herself, ideas, and the few approximate measurements she had made.

Erin gazed with determination at the falls, the boulders, and the sandstone ledges separating each of the levels as they descended to the lake. She finally gave in and allowed her eyes to wander to Alex Butler. He was busily plowing through underbrush, climbing ledges, leaping from boulders, and taking notes. My, such activity. It tickled her immensely, for she herself was spending twice her normal time on her own notes, pretending to be busy just because he was there.

When Alex returned, she was still sitting on the log, her pad on her knees. She saw that his hair was all tumbled and he had acquired a nasty scratch on the back of one hand.

He frowned down at her. "So, you think Van is right?" He ran both hands through his hair, taming it, and caught sight of the glistening scratch. He ignored it.

"Don't you?" She closed her notebook and noticed with a pang that his face was attractively flushed from exertion. "I think it's fantastic here."

"I didn't say it wasn't fantastic." There was room on the log and he sat down beside her. He picked up a dry twig and noisily began to snap it into pieces.

"But not for a house—is that what you mean?" Erin offered.

"Let's face it, Ms. Kelly. It would be one hell of a struggle to build anything here with all those boulders scattered around, and to escape the boulders, you move downstream and get flooding. It will also be damp. You'd have to rip out a flock of trees to get any sunlight. Now— you wouldn't want to do *that*, would you?"

His easy smile caught her by surprise. It erased the stiff mask he'd been wearing and softened the hard planes and lines of his dark face. Erin blinked up at him, unaware of the sudden roses in her cheeks, knowing only that her heart was pumping blood through her body at an alarming rate.

"On the contrary," she answered. "With a minimum of clearing, I think a house could have sun almost as long as it's available. Address it 30–60 degrees to the south, naturally"—she gave him a disarming smile—"and put it right about there." She pointed toward the giant boulder beside the creek.

Alex Butler looked at the spot politely, then looked back at her. "No one could move *that* boulder," he declared firmly, as though that were the end of it. "Besides, a house anywhere near it would be too close to the creek."

"I wasn't thinking of moving the boulder." She tried another smile on him. "I was thinking of using it as a fulcrum. The house could balance on it." That idea, miraculously, had just come to her.

"Thereby putting the house so close to the falls that you'd have to incorporate them, too." There was quiet amusement in his black eyes, as though he were dealing with a complete idiot but wouldn't let on.

"*Bingo*. I may do just that." Her irritation was sprouting, but it was irritation with herself more than with him.

Erin resented that he could be so cool and polite, no doubt having forgotten he'd ever wanted to kiss her. She, however, was enticed by everything about him. His blue-black hair, with bits of dried leaves clinging in it, his tall, rangy body; his capable-looking brown hands—even the dark shadow on his jaw seemed to excite her.

"Ah," he said, "another Fallingwater." Now he really was laughing at her. He was close enough so she could see that his eyes were not black at all but brown—a deep brown with tawny flecks in them. "Another Frank Lloyd Wright," Alex added as he grinned.

Erin took a long, controlled breath and managed to

remain calm. He was referring to her idol, the century's greatest organic architect, and to his most famous creation, Fallingwater, a house build over a waterfall. Alex was intimating that she was going to copy it.

"I assure you, Mr. Butler, that if I take this commission, the house I design will be my own. Completely. Imitation doesn't appeal to me, and I can visualize a house built on that boulder with a room cantilevered over the stream. Or perhaps an enclosed walkway over it leading to another wing."

He was still grinning and as hard as she tried to preserve her serenity, it was slipping away.

"I don't like condescension." Erin's lips felt stiff. "Are you laughing because you think I can't design a house over a waterfall?"

He stood up and stretched, making the muscles under his jeans tighten.

"Well, Mrs. Kelly—"

"*Ms.* Kelly," she snapped.

There was a sudden hesitant look on his face, though he was still cool and controlled. "Listen, Kelly, my aim has always been to please my clients, not to have them swept away and drowned." He shook his head. "Lady, I wouldn't touch this shaky project with a fifty-foot pole."

"Good. You don't know what a relief it is to hear you say that."

Erin rose, her chin tilted regally, and started for the path to the bluff. She had to get away from him. She was angry, yes, but more than that, she was being overwhelmed by his raw masculinity.

"Go back to your mall, Mr. Butler. It so happens—" She caught her tongue between her teeth to still it, but when she let go, it rattled on anyway. "I'd rather create one or two glorious buildings in my lifetime than spawn one monstrosity after another—like *your* third-rate architects."

Erin gasped at her own audacity and, at the same time, stepped into a chuck hole. She would have sprawled flat on her face if Alex Butler hadn't caught her tightly by the upper arm. She saw his glittering gaze through the corner of her eye, and she couldn't look away. She could only stare at him, embarrassed and a little frightened as he spoke.

"My God, you're arrogant. Arrogant and sassy and disrespectful." He roughly spun her around so she faced him and both his hands held her fast. "Don't you know you should be more reverent?"

She saw then that he wasn't even angry. His mouth tilted at one corner as he tried not to laugh, which meant she had been about as effective as a gnat attacking a lion. Her eyes lingered on his lips. What would they taste like? she wondered again. She moistened her own in unconscious preparation, then breathed a long, soft sigh.

"And in addition to all that"—his voice was husky and suddenly serious—"you're sexy, Erin Kelly." She felt such a sudden torrent of fire between their bodies that her legs went wobbly. What in the world was happening? They had been squabbling just moments ago.

Alex's hand cupped her chin, raising her face to his own as his mouth came closer and closer until she felt the gentle pressure of his lips. So gentle. Almost a question.

When she didn't pull away, and when she slowly moved her hands over his chest, feeling his heavy heartbeat and the hard, solid wall of his muscles, his kiss gradually began to change. His mouth tightly sealed her own, and one hand slipped down to her throat while the other caressed her arm. When his fingertips stroked her silky skin, Erin's breathing quickened and a little shiver raced up her spine.

But it was no good, and no good could possibly come of

it. It was exactly what she had determined not to do. But his mouth was so delicious in its slow, lingering kiss; just the way she had imagined it might be. And Alex smelled wonderful, his skin and hair scented with the leather of his jacket and the pine from the woods around them.

She turned her head, breaking off the kiss. "Alex . . ." She rested her head against his chest for a moment, listening to his rapidly beating heart and wondering wildly where it would all end.

He tilted her chin and took Erin's mouth once more. This time his kiss was piercing and hungry—a fierce, sudden hunger—and she enjoyed the electrifying shock.

She felt his arms go beneath hers, felt his hands lock together behind her, and then her feet left the ground. Erin was lifted up until her face was nearly level with his own, her breasts crushed against her chest, his one hand behind her head and deep in her hair as he searched her mouth.

She responded eagerly. She wanted to press her small, soft body to Alex's until there was no space left between them. Her fingertips slowly savored the thick silkiness of his hair and the way it curved darkly against his neck and temples, then moved on to the roughness of his cheeks and jaw, an exciting contrast to her own smooth skin. All the while, Erin's willing mouth treasured his thrusting, exploring kisses. She answered them with wild hungry little caresses of her own.

But deep inside, she was despairing. This was the first and the last time she would do such a thing; she shouldn't—couldn't—let it continue. Just then her thoughts were overcome by a new burst of sensation. Her breasts were suddenly full and pulsing, aching for Alex to claim them, and there was an insistent hot throbbing current flowing through her body, warming her and leading her toward a peak of exquisite torment . . .

No. She grabbed his shoulders and pushed him, turning away from his kiss. "Alex, please stop." She shook her head.

He allowed her body to slide down slowly, touching every part of him, until her toes touched the ground.

"Whew." It was a little half-whistle. "You're something else, Ms. Kelly."

His hands were still locked behind her and she gently tried to free herself. "If you'll just . . . unhand me. I really must go now."

"My God." he was laughing down at her. "Is that all you have to say?"

"I usually don't do this sort of thing. Really, it was . . . a mistake."

Alex released her, and when she started off, he followed along.

"I want to see you again. How about tonight?"

Erin's heart had been pounding so wildly she was breathless. "I'm sorry. I can't . . ."

"I suppose there's someone else?"

"No. It's just that my work takes up all my time and, besides, I don't want to . . . get close to anyone just now."

"That suits me fine, Kelly." The deep voice was practically in her ear. "We can have a hell of a fling without getting close. I don't hanker after closeness, either."

She spun around and faced him, her astonished eyes reflecting the blue-green of sky and water.

"You certainly say what you think."

"Don't *you?*" His lips held a mocking smile, and she couldn't deny it.

"Touché."

Continuing up the path, Erin had to dig in her toes and cling to branches to support herself. She was unsettled. Not by his words—of course he wanted her in bed—but for the second time now she had seen the faintest trace of sorrow in his eyes before it was hidden. A glimmer of tragedy. She almost said, I know, love, I know. Everything will be all right . . . But maybe it wouldn't be all right.

She was puffing when she got to the top of the bluff, and Mighty Mouse had never looked so good, dirty and scruffy as he was. She strode up to Carl's long-ago gift, a gift meant to take her mind off his treachery, kicked the mud from her boots, and slid behind the wheel. Alex closed the door for her.

"Kelly . . ."

"Yes?"

"I shouldn't have come on to you like that about a fling. I'm sorry. And don't be embarrassed about . . . anything. You're okay. You're a lady. I can see that." He put a hand on her shoulder and she knew a bonfire wouldn't warm her nearly so much as his words and comforting touch.

"You're okay, too, Alex." Her eyes were large and luminous against her flushed skin. "I don't know why I can't behave better when I'm around you. I'm sorry . . ." She sighed as she turned the key and Mighty Mouse roared to life.

She was backing up slowly to turn around and head downhill when Alex frowned. He held up a warning hand.

"What is it?" She rolled down the window.

"You've got a flat. It's a damned good thing it happened here instead of somewhere along I-79. I can have your spare on in a jiffy."

She turned off the ignition, got out, and slammed the door. Erin didn't need to say a word; he read her face.

"You don't have a spare."

"It might get me one or two miles." She felt completely weighed down. Getting a spare was one of the things she'd meant to do before leaving Chicago, but she had forgotten and everything had been fine so far.

"Ah, Kelly." His eyes moved sadly over the neglected car.

Actually, she hated the little beast in spite of its fine performance. It had been a shiny, powerful little bullet when she chose it, a symbol of hope. Hope that Carl would change and all would be well with their marriage, but not so. He had tended the needs of the Saab more carefully than her own, and after she left him, she'd ignored the car shamefully. Of course she had maintenance work done when it could no longer be put off, but otherwise she paid as little attention to it as possible. It was a reminder of everything she wanted to forget, but she couldn't afford a new car and was afraid of used ones.

Alex reached in and got the key to lock the doors. "I'll take you wherever you want to go and I'll send two men back in the chopper to get the car." He was leading her to the shiny yellow helicopter.

"Why, that's awfully kind of you. I'll reimburse you, of course." And it would be a fortune, no doubt. It looked like her sins against Mighty Mouse were coming home to roost at last.

"I won't accept money, but . . ." His eyes swept over her as he leered wickedly. "Sorry, Kelly, I couldn't resist that."

It was much too noisy to talk above the clatter of the chopper, so Erin just sat back and enjoyed the view. It was early March and the land was already beginning to turn green. She liked the way the swollen silver streams meandered below and the way the weeping willows clustered here and there along their banks, a soft green-gold against the brown earth. Everything was so different, so beautiful from this height.

She watched Alex's hands on the controls, thinking

how different he was now from their first volcanic meeting, warm and friendly and helpful. A little shiver moved along her skin as she remembered his kisses.

Erin shifted uncomfortably in her seat. Just because a man was handsome and smelled and tasted wonderful was no reason to get all worked up. All that faded eventually and one was left with what was most important: the way the man thought and acted and was. She knew. She had had firsthand experience.

But, watching him from the corner of her eye, Erin felt like a young girl again. He was big and dark and seemed dangerous, dangerous because she was so attracted to him. She had wanted him to make love to her back by the lake . . .

She fidgeted, folding her arms across her breasts. What was it about her that drew her to men who were either unattainable or who were basically third-rate beneath a veneer of success?

First there had been Nicholas van Rijn, a ridiculous twenty-one years her senior. Next came Carlton Kelly, the thief and womanizer. And now Alex Butler, a man with values that were very different from hers, a man who'd just admitted that a quick fling would satisfy him. Yes, he had apologized, and his apology had warmed her at the time, but she wanted a man a step above that. A fling—Humph. It was tacky, just like his mall . . .

Erin felt his hand on her arm and looked over to where he was pointing. The city was in the distance and she felt a swell of pride that it was her city, this dazzle of silver and diamonds on the horizon. It was sun on glass and metal—the elegant spires of Pittsburgh—and on the glistening waters of the Allegheny, the Monongahela, and the Ohio, the three rivers forming the Golden Triangle that was the very heart of the city.

She had seen Pittsburgh from the air many times, but

never before had she noticed its masculinity. It was a city of iron and steel with buildings that were tall and strong, giants scraping the clouds. Their skins gleamed gold and rust and pewter and their lines were straight, hard and uncompromising. Male beauty. Erin shivered with the delight of it before she realized it wasn't the city that was making her feel this way.

Oh, no. Not this man, she thought, for up until this moment, she'd been rational. Please, Lord . . . But Erin knew it was too late for such a prayer. Wave after wave of tantalizing sensations swept over her, leaving her soft and trembling and ready for nothing but love. Her breath caught at the thought.

Erin wanted him to possess her completely. She wanted his arms and his legs wrapped about her, wanted Alex to capture and probe her mouth with his kisses once more, wanted him deep within her . . .

She bit down hard on her lower lip and noticed her hands. They were clenched in her lap, the nails gouging her palms. Oh, no . . . The incredible but lovely thought of having a baby with him had just occurred to her. Erin stared straight ahead, desperately trying to control her tumultuous feelings.

Good God, she thought, it had happened again. She'd fallen in love. Maybe not at first sight, but close to it. No matter how hard she might struggle against it, deep inside she knew the battle was hopeless.

Alex gave her a happy smile just then, a brief dazzle of white against his dark skin, and a comradely pat on the knee.

Feeling unbearably warm, Erin unzipped her survival jacket. She really was jumping the gun. A *baby*. How silly. She wouldn't go to bed with him, of course. She had been reared a certain way and it had stuck. She was old-fashioned, and wasn't about to change her ways now.

As they flew over Glenshaw she pointed out Strawberry Way and her old farmhouse set in the middle of ten acres. Alex competently set the helicopter down and then helped her out from beneath the whirring blades. Erin shouted her thanks and gave him her brightest smile.

She waited until the yellow bird had disappeared from sight, then she went inside and collapsed on the sofa. Alex was gone, but she was still held in the spell of his dark magnetism. The Corcoran genes were riding again, just as she had told Deirdre. Erin knew what she *should* do, but how could she possibly forget that this afternoon had ever happened?

Chapter Four

Erin finally forced herself to the telephone. She had to call Deirdre and report in.

"Hi, love, I'm home. Anything exciting I should know about?" She congratulated herself on sounding perfectly normal.

"Darling, why are you home? I thought you were coming back to the office. Mr. Phillips called with that tax and bond info you wanted, and Margaret Murray wants to talk about the local codes for that shelling-out job you might do for her. I told them you'd call back. Are you all right?" In Deirdre's typical style, her words all came out in a single breath.

Erin wouldn't lie to her sister; she just wouldn't tell her what had happened at Laurel Lake. Deirdre would push her at Alex Butler, and when Erin had to make every effort to keep her mind off the man, that was the last thing she needed.

"I don't feel so hot," Erin said truthfully. Her stomach felt as though a lead basketball had landed there. "And I didn't know anything was scheduled. I just want to rest a bit." And sleep for a month and then maybe everything would be solved when she awoke, she told herself.

"I thought you looked a little peaked recently. Take a long nap now, darling, and have a good dinner. Maybe you should take vitamins."

When she finally hung up, Erin stood looking about her kitchen. It was a comforting room, spacious yet cozy, with plants on the windowsills, hand-woven baskets on one wall, and her copper pans close at hand on a pegboard above the stove. Wonder of wonders, it had a big fireplace, and she'd put her grandfather's old clock on the stone mantel. Erin could forget her problems here, and the first step was to get the kettle on for tea and start the fire. There was nothing quite so comforting as rocking in front of a good fire, sipping a mug of Earl Grey.

She bustled about and was soon enjoying the warmth and coziness of hearth and tea, thinking it would be nicer still if there were some living thing to greet her when she came home from work. A cat, maybe. She loved dogs, but a dog would be too dependent for her irregular hours.

The thought of Alex Butler swept over her like a tidal wave just then, swamping the dog and cat: Alex coming home to her, striding into the kitchen and lifting her off her feet to give her a spine-tingling kiss.

Leaping up, Erin paced around the kitchen table and tried to take her mind off him. After circling the kitchen three times, she decided she would cook. She would make a couple of casseroles, bake some bread, and roll out some pie shells. This blessed old kitchen had not only a fireplace but a huge freezer, which she hadn't as yet taken full advantage of.

She was happily sautéing leeks and mushrooms for a chicken casserole when the telephone rang. It was Van. He was back from California and eager to take her up to see Laurel Lake.

"Van, I've been there already. I went up just today and it *is* beautiful, just as you said."

"Ah." There was a short pause before he asked, "Dare I hope, then, that you will accept the commission?"

Erin continued to stir the mushrooms and leeks in the

bubbling butter. She added a bit of flour and nervously stirred it to a perfect thickness.

"I'd like to do it, Van. I really would, but . . ." She breathed a long sigh.

"What's your objection to Alex?" said the voice in her ear. She could imagine Van's blue eyes narrowing.

"He's already told you, Van. We disagree—clash, really—and we have very different ideas about architecture. That mall he's doing north of Glenshaw is just about the ugliest thing I've ever seen."

"But in this case, my dear," Van said soothingly, "you will be the architect."

"Yes, but I have no doubts that he'll hinder me and object to anything new I might want to do. And I'm sure he holds his architects on a tight rein. Completely under his thumb. I can't work that way." And yet Alex was warm and friendly and generous, sending men up to fix her car and return it to her.

She was stirring away as she talked and now began to add a dollop of wine. She accidentally sloshed nearly half a cup. *Damn.* She tried to spoon it out.

"I'm used to just the opposite," she continued. "My builders must do what *I* want."

"Perhaps Alex will be much more amenable than you imagine."

"*Ha.*" She was remembering the hesitant look on Alex's face as he eyed the huge granite boulder, and how the look had turned to condescension. One image led to another, and then she was remembering the taste of his kisses and how she'd wanted him to be part of her . . .

Erin had turned up the heat under the pan and she suddenly noticed that the beautiful vegetables were burning around the edges.

"I propose we go to the site Sunday," Van was saying. "I'll give Alex a call right now." She had started to sput-

ter an excuse, but then realized she had no legitimate reason not to go. Drat the man. Why in the world was he
insisting on Alex Butler? "We can stop for you around
one," he continued, "and perhaps then we can come to a
decision."

She came to a decision of her own just then.

"All right. Why not? It sounds like a good idea. I'll see
you then."

What she meant to do was simple, actually. Van had
given her complete control over the design; she would
insist on building the house right beside Otter Run and
using that magnificent boulder as a fulcrum. Alex Butler,
being as obstinate as she was, would back off. Hadn't he
already said he wouldn't touch the project with a fifty-
foot pole? Erin would then be free to choose Roberto
Strata as her builder, and everything would be fine. Well,
almost everything. There was an empty spot in her
heart . . .

She went to the room she used as her office, switched
on the light, and opened the bottom drawer of her filing
cabinet. It contained things she hadn't looked at for
years, and if the sketch she wanted wasn't there, she had
no idea where to look.

But it *was* there, and it was good. Erin only wished the
satisfaction she derived from looking at it could take away
the leaden feeling in her stomach. It was miserable, wanting a man and at the same time running from him.

The car that arrived precisely at one o'clock Sunday afternoon wasn't the Mercedes sedan. It was a limousine, a
long, black, elegant machine that looked as though it once
had belonged to an Arab sheikh. Erin's eyes widened for an
instant at the ostentation. Then Van gave her a warm kiss
on the cheek, took her elbow, and led her down the brick

walk to the car. Alex, too, had gotten out, and he gave her a friendly but noncommittal nod.

"Morning, Ms. Kelly."

"Good morning, Mr. Butler." Her eyes were grateful. "Thanks again." When the Saab arrived Friday night, she had tried to call him three times to thank him, and was finally told he was out of town. Now she smiled at him before hastily directing her glance to the young woman seated in the plush maroon interior of the car.

"Hello, I'm Cecile van Rijn." As the girl held out a welcoming hand, Erin saw that Van's daughter had indeed grown into a beauty.

"Hello, Cecile." Erin returned the greeting and settled in the seat beside her. As the two began to chatter brightly, getting to know each other, Erin was dismayed to feel a twinge of envy.

Cecile's hair was fine and smooth with every strand in place, not a cloud of unruly auburn curls like Erin's. Her blue eyes had a cool, level gaze like her father's, a bit frosty and commanding. They weren't too big or too widely spaced, nor were they a color that was neither blue nor green, like her own.

That's enough, Erin told herself sternly, remembering how she had been intimidated by Cecile van Rijn's good looks even when she was sixteen and Cecile only ten.

Today she had thrown on her second-best work clothes, a scant step above blue jeans and a survival jacket. Erin knew what she was in for—mud, brambles, and rocks—and she wanted to be prepared.

Now she wondered what Cecile was thinking as her cool blue eyes moved slowly over the worn dark green corduroys tucked into tall brown boots, her white shirt and burgundy corduroy jacket. Erin knew the jacket was a striking foil for her hair, and, although she was presentable, she was unmistakably in work clothes.

Cecile herself was in crisp straight-leg blue denims, gum shoes, a wheat-colored ragg sweater that matched her hair, and a khaki jacket. Decidedly preppy, but effective nonetheless.

The long car hummed quietly along. Erin wondered if Van had rented it for the occasion; after all, who would need both a large Mercedes sedan and this? Now she had second thoughts as she listened to the conversation.

Van, on the seat facing her, was expounding at length on corporate finances, the stock market, and foreign-exchange rates while Alex, sitting beside him, listened and joined in with intelligent comments. Cecile, she noticed, smiled at Alex much of the time while listening to her father. It was clear that she adored and admired "Daddy."

Erin's ears suddenly pricked up at what Van was saying. He had purchased Laurel Lake ten years ago, and now its value had at least quintupled. He was considering either subdividing the land and selling the plots himself or selling it whole to a developer.

"Oh, Van." It was her first entry into their conversation. "Surely you wouldn't spoil all that beautiful wilderness. What about your own site?"

He smiled. "Of course I would keep a hundred acres or so for myself."

"But then you'd be looking across the lake at roads and telephone poles and rows of houses." Erin couldn't help it. She shuddered. *"Ugh."*

The three of them laughed at her uninhibited exclamation of distaste, then Alex said, "Ms. Kelly likes trees, Van. In this case I have to agree with her, for once."

When his amused brown eyes turned on her, that same exciting current Erin had felt before crackled between them. Her legs and arms grew limp, and she knew she wouldn't have had the strength to pick up a feather or crumple a tissue just then. Not to save her soul.

She carefully avoided Alex's eyes for the remainder of the trip and chatted with Cecile. The girl was twenty-one now and so in love with life that it made Erin a bit tired just to hear all her plans. Had she herself ever been so young and exuberant? she thought wistfully. She knew she had; it was just that Carl had taken a lot out of her.

After they arrived at Laurel Lake and reached the site, Cecile playfully caught Alex's hand and took him off "to see something special." Erin's eyes followed them and she noticed that Alex had gone willingly.

"Now, then, you already have something to show me?" Van said.

She nodded and removed her sketch from the cardboard tube she carried. "It's a house project I did in college. I liked the feel of it for this setting."

Van took it and perused it silently.

"Of course it's too fragile-looking for this setting," she explained, "because there's too much glass." Besides, Erin didn't think an ethereal-looking house would be appropriate for Nicholas van Rijn. "But I rather liked the terraces and the low, straight lines hugging the earth."

When he didn't say anything but continued to study the sketch, she ventured, "I think it should be bold, Van, bold and primitive, as if it's part of the earth."

His eyes were admiring. "You're right. Absolutely right."

"Of course I'm right." She gave him a playful smile, and his own smile was playful in return.

"Erin, you're adorable. I warn you—I want to take you home with me."

She got to work then, taking out her pencil and pad. Sitting on the same log where she'd so recently sat with Alex, Erin looked around her: a frothy curtain of white

water tumbled over the falls, then rushed headlong over
the jagged rocks and on down to the lake. Black, naked
branches contrasted with the pale russet and green of the
leaves that had fallen and those that still lived. Then, too,
there were the rhododendrons and the laurel and pine
trees, the buff sandstone ledges, and the dark boulders—
humped, massive reminders of the Ice Age. Prehistoric.

Ideas sprang to her mind so rapidly that Erin's fingers
could barely keep up with them. Set against the music
from the falls and the creek, a house took form on the
paper before her. As it grew, she knew it was good. Better, she felt, than anything she had ever done. Erin had it
balancing on the rock—her rock—and she even had one
bedroom wing soaring out, cantilevered over the wild torrent of the falls.

Van had looked over her shoulder from time to time and
when he stopped behind her again, she spoke.

"What do you think?" She was flushed with triumph.

"Very nice, my dear. I believe it will do."

She looked up at his bland countenance. Not even a
glimmer of excitement showed in his face. Quintus
Corcoran had once called his young colleague a cold, stolid
Dutchman. She saw that coldness now, but she hid her
disappointment.

"Here they come," Van said. "Let's see what Cecile
thinks."

"It's marvelous," his daughter crowed. "Hot damn.
Oh, Daddy, I *love* it." Her blue eyes were dancing with
excitement but, then, they had been even before she
viewed the sketch. Erin promptly stifled her thoughts.

"Let me see." Alex took the sketch from Cecile's
hands and Erin was pleased at the genuine interest in his
eyes. "Very nice, Ms. Kelly." He was nodding, taking in
every detail. "I'm impressed."

"Thank you." If a bolt had come out of the blue just

then, Erin wouldn't have been as surprised, but she had only a moment to bask in the glow his words gave her.

"I see you have the house placed on top of that boulder, after all." He looked at the rock and back at her. "But is it stable enough to act as a fulcrum, Ms. Kelly? Personally, I would never use it as part of the structure. It puts the foundation walls damned close to the falls, don't you think?"

"Approximately eighteen feet," she snapped. "It's perfectly adequate leeway."

"Adequate only if there's no undercutting of the ledge under the falls. We don't know how fast the falls are receding, do we, Van?" Van shrugged.

"I can see no substantial difference between the way it looks now and the way it looked ten years ago. But no tests have been made. Why worry about such a thing, Alex?"

"Of course we'll have the proper tests made to reassure us all of the boulder's stability," Erin interjected coolly. "I'll call out a team of engineers to do that and to check the falls for erosion."

"I'll use my own engineers, if you don't mind, Ms. Kelly."

Erin shrugged. Things were going exactly as she'd thought they might, but she wished she could feel glad about it.

"The stream will flood," Alex was scowling. "Debris could damage the foundation walls."

"They'll be sufficiently thick to withstand it."

"*How* thick?" Alex asked aggressively.

"Two feet." She glared at him.

"Not enough. Make it three. Of course, you realize the site might not even support the concentrated load of the building?"

"You must think I'm a beginner, Mr. Butler."

"Not at all, Ms. Kelly, but I do think you might be better off not imitating Frank Lloyd Wright."

"How *dare* you?" Erin had a short fuse on that subject. In the past, when anyone had tried to soothe her pain over Carl's treachery with that terrible old bromide about imitation being flattery, she had hurled the master architect's words at them: "Imitation is insult, not flattery."

Her eyes flashed angry sparks as they locked on his but she was really more hurt than angry. In fact, he couldn't have hurt her more if he'd intended to. Forgotten were his kindness with the car and his kisses.

"Oh, hell," Alex said.

"Now, my friends," Van said, "let's be judicious about this."

Cecile seemed to be enjoying the scene.

"I *meant* imitating Wright's stunt with the waterfall," Alex growled, "not his design. Don't fly off the handle." He jammed his hands in his pockets and scowled at the boulder.

"Well, now that that small misunderstanding is taken care of, my dear, will you accept the commission?"

"Mr. Butler is right about many things," she answered stiffly. "That boulder and the erosion of the ledge under the falls must be checked. We also need test borings for the load capacity and soil content, and a plane-table survey so we can identify these rock outcroppings. Oh, yes, and a record of every tree and boulder here."

"It shall be done."

"I hope the news is all good," Cecile added. "I love the sketch."

"You hear, Erin? Cecile wants the house. Now, let's suppose that all the 'ifs' fall into place and a house is feasible on this site. Will you work with Alex?"

Erin forced a laugh. "You've seen the problem, Van, how we are together." Alex had moved off downhill and was staring past them to the great boulder. "I love this area and I think I can give you the house you want, but I'm just not sure about . . . him."

"I know." Van cocked his head, giving her a sympathetic smile. Erin suddenly saw in him the man she had once fallen for with all the pain and sweetness that accompany the first love of adolescence. Damn. She did want to please him, and it wasn't as if she and the builder, whoever he might be, were going to be collaborating on the World Trade Center. Only a little house, as Deirdre had said. A house of relative simplicity when compared with Fallingwater's complexity.

She was probably making too much of an issue about it, but Alex's questions *had* been probing. He was no fool. He was obviously a competent builder who understood all the potential problems and negative aspects of the site.

Alex was slowly walking toward them, his dark, searching eyes taking in everything. Admit it, Erin thought, you're intrigued by the idea of working with him.

But he was so negative about everything, picking out nothing but the difficulties, whereas she could think only of the challenges and the exciting results.

Erin suddenly had a startling insight: she was as bad as he. She was negative where he was concerned, thinking only about the difficulties in working with him and ignoring the challenges and the possible achievement.

She needed time to digest this interesting new viewpoint but Van was waiting for an answer.

"Well, I suppose I can manage with Alex," she said finally.

"My sweet." She was suddenly pulled into Van's arms and he was giving her a hard, exuberant kiss on the cheek. Alex walked up just then and his dark eyes flickered impassively over the two of them.

"The datum, Ms. Kelly. How do I find the datum in this jungle?"

"Go right through that patch of mountain laurel, Mr. Butler." Erin smiled at him sweetly. "If you climb that ledge to your left, you should find your datum."

"What's a 'datum'?" Cecile wanted to know.

"It's a level line or a point used as a reference in measuring the elevation," said her father. Erin was impressed. Nicholas van Rijn, it seemed, knew many things. "Alex, wait." He grabbed the builder's arm before Alex moved off in search of the datum. "What about you? Can I count on you?"

"Only if she can come up with the answers, Van."

Alex was addressing himself to Van as though Erin weren't there, and she wondered why he was acting so rudely. She rather hoped, childishly, that he was jealous of Van's kiss. Alex had no way of knowing it had been merely a fatherly peck on her cheek.

"I can give you a decent house here," Alex continued. "Something that can take everything this terrain and this climate can throw at you—we're in a snow belt here, you know. But that doesn't include jutting the house over a waterfall. I'd say no to that. Put the house back in some nice spot where you can look at the falls without being clobbered by them. Believe me, there will be trouble enough building on this site without going out looking for it."

Van heard only what interested him. "Are you saying that if it's possible you will accept?" Both men seemed to have forgotten Erin as they drifted off toward the waterfall, deep in conversation.

"Hi." Cecile had been off somewhere briefly and was now back. "I hope it all works out."

Erin nodded. "Now we do the tests and wait for the results."

"It's strange, though."

"What's strange?"

"My father has had this land for ten years and never once considered building a house here. Not until now."

"Maybe he just likes the idea of an old friend designing it."

Cecile shrugged. "Maybe." It was clear she thought no such thing. Her blue eyes sought out the men as she and Erin talked.

"What a hunk of man," she said. She took out a cigarette, lit it, and continued to watch Alex. "Did Daddy tell you it was my idea to hire Alex?"

"No, he didn't. I was wondering about that. Is there any particular reason?" But she already knew the answer.

Cecile laughed. "Need you ask? Just look at him—he's *gorgeous*."

Erin had to agree, but she only said, "He'll do, I suppose."

Alex was almost a head taller than Van, and as they moved about, his lean ranginess was completely at home with the wild surroundings. Van, on the other hand, looked like what he was: the highly groomed, well-tailored president and major shareholder of a large corporation. He seemed out of place away from his desk and his boardroom.

"I must say, I'm glad you're so lukewarm about Alex. My plan is to net him this summer, and it all hinges on you."

"On me?" Worse and worse.

"Well, if you have the right answers, then Alex will do the building and I'll get to see him all the time. The rest is easy."

"That's a rather poor reason for selecting a builder, don't you think?" Erin looked at the girl sternly, but Cecile merely smiled.

"I thought it was inspired. It's not as though he's a

dummy, you know. Oh, well," she said, shrugging, "if this idea falls through, I'll just have to think of something else." Her smile was dazzling, confident. "I'll manage. He's as good as mine." She snapped her fingers.

"I suppose that means you don't really care about my sketch or what kind of house is built here. As long as *he* builds it." Erin was close to exploding.

"You're wrong. I love your sketch, and if I'm lucky, I'll have both the house *and* Alex. If my father has taught me anything, it's that a van Rijn always gets what he or she wants."

"Admirable." It seemed that Erin's major difficulty was about to be solved; Alex Butler would be gobbled up whole by this remarkable young woman.

"It sounds insufferable, doesn't it?"

"Rather." Erin broke into a grin despite her irritation. She liked this young snip. How did you *not* like someone who loved your work? But it would be jolly to take her down a peg or two. "How do you plan to go about this . . . conquest?"

"I'm not sure. Since he's so elusive, I'll probably just try for togetherness at first. You know, let him get comfortable with me. I don't want to scare him off."

"Why do you say he's elusive?"

"When a man's thirty-four and no one's gotten him, he's elusive. I've heard he's had one true love—some bittersweet romance—and scads of women since."

"Flings?" Erin asked darkly, using Alex's own word.

"Probably." Cecile gave a casual shrug. "I'll even settle for a fling if all else fails."

"Well, he sounds like bad news to me," Erin said stiffly. "Are you sure you want someone who plays around like that?"

"When that 'someone' looks like Alex Butler," Cecile laughed, "why not?"

The look of bored amusement on her lovely face said that she wouldn't expect a provincial like Erin Kelly to understand such things—uncontrollable passions that demanded satisfaction without the benefit of matrimony.

Oh, little girl, if you only knew, Erin thought, but she refused to give in to those passions herself. She meant to exercise fully the discipline that every good architect must have, but she also knew that it would still be hard to say no to Alex when she wanted to say yes. At least Cecile's gossip about him would make it a bit easier. Scads of women, indeed!

Chapter Five

❧

The days that followed were jam packed with work. Erin was busy consulting for a proposed clinic in Oakland, and she made the trip to Natrona Heights to inspect the site for the new hospital wing. Both Van and Deirdre were touting her prowess, and, having won the Esperanza competition in Mexico, she was rapidly acquiring more clients. Erin was riding a crest and it couldn't have come at a better time—it helped to keep her mind off Alex Butler.

When all the Laurel test results came in, in her favor, Erin was bright-eyed and anxious to start. Three weeks of happy activity, with Alex pushed into the background, had put her in fine fettle. She could cope with anything and her energy was at a peak.

She would come home from Shadyside, eat a light meal, and sit down at the drawing board, sometimes until midnight or one A.M. Now that Alex's negative questions had all been answered, she was running on sheer exuberance and triumph.

From the day she had first seen the Laurel terrain, Erin knew how she would utilize the boulder, the ledges, and the falls. Her woman's intuition had told her that it could be done. Woman's intuition. She laughed at the thought. How Alex would grumble and scowl at that.

Using a different colored pencil for each floor, she had sketched out several north-south and east-west perspectives, as well as several straight-on views, picking from them the ones she liked best.

Her house of glass was taking on new life. It was becoming a bold structure of redwood, stone, and stucco set in the cascading valley in such a way as to take advantage of cheerful sunlight all day long; it would be a house that would commune with the forest and the stream beside it, a house with a graceful bedroom wing soaring out over the falls.

When she took the drawings to Shadyside and Deirdre saw them on the board, she gasped. "Darling, it's magnificent! So woodsy and earthy somehow. Positively striking!"

Erin beamed. It was; it was earth architecture.

"But are you sure it's the sort of thing Nicholas wants, dear? He's always been such a city person—why, he even used to hate getting his feet wet! He must have gone through a complete personality change since the old days."

"He approved the first sketch."

"Well, wonders never cease. It's just too marvelous for words." She leaned closer and peered at the rendering. "Won't that room over the creek fall down?"

Erin laughed. "Heavens, I *hope* not. It's built with a cantilever, a beam extended beyond its support."

"Oh, I see," said Deirdre brightly, not seeing at all.

"Think of a branch growing from a tree trunk," Erin explained, "or an outstretched arm. It's completely natural-looking and it's based on a natural principle. It doesn't need vertical support because . . ." But Deirdre was fidgeting and seemed glad to answer the telephone and return to her paperwork. Erin grinned. They really did complement each other, neither wanting to do the work that pleased the other.

Six weeks to the day after Erin had first seen Laurel, she

delivered her completed drawings to Van in his Oakland office. Alex was to be there as well, but he hadn't yet arrived when Van sat at his desk, his narrowed eyes scanning every detail. Erin held her breath.

"It's exactly right, my dear," he said finally. "Just what I had in mind."

Erin expected him to continue talking about the house, but he merely sat back in his big leather chair and eyed her. She blinked and smiled, thinking that she had to be wrong, but she wasn't. Van was definitely eyeing her.

She cleared her throat. "Well, what changes would you like me to make?"

"Why, none, my sweet. Unless there are some you have in mind—anything you want will please me."

Erin could only stare at him. Clients always wanted changes. "Van, this is *your* house."

But his mind, it seemed, was not on architecture.

"It was most unfortunate I . . . had to disappoint you so long ago, Erin. Have you ever forgiven me for that?" When her mouth opened in astonishment, he smiled and continued. "You see, I knew all along how you felt about me."

"Van." She laughed. "You were . . ." She had been about to say he had been old enough to be her father, but she caught herself just in time; he was *still* old enough to be her father. "Surely you weren't interested in a sixteen-year-old kid?"

"You were a lovely young woman, Erin. A sweet and innocent nymph. In many ways you still are."

Her eyes widened in alarm. "Van, I was gawky and wore braces and had too many freckles." His blue eyes seemed those of a moonstruck lover, and she couldn't believe he was talking to her this way.

"Now it's I"—his voice dropped intimately—"who feel toward you as you once felt about me."

Erin started to protest, but he rose and came around his desk to draw her up out of the chair.

He tilted her chin. "My dear, why is it so unusual that I have fallen in love with the brilliant, beautiful woman you've become?"

"Oh, Van." His words were terribly upsetting, and could only complicate her position further.

"Now you are free and I am free."

Erin shook her head. "Van, I'm so sorry . . ."

His hands were on her shoulders and she was looking up at him, dewy-eyed, when Alex walked in.

"It seems I'm intruding," he said, "but your secretary said to walk right in."

Alex's gaze took in what appeared to be an intimate moment, then moved lazily over her navy corduroy skirt, cream shirt, and high-heeled leather boots.

"No, you're not intruding at *all*," she protested. Alex looked at her skeptically, and when she remembered his "scads of women," Erin decided it really didn't matter what he thought. Not in the least.

The three sat down then, and Van's competent secretary brought in fresh coffee.

"Now, then, Alex," Van said, "as you know, all systems are go, and Erin has just shown me her sketches. I'm satisfied." He handed them across the gleaming walnut surface of his desk to Alex.

Erin was suddenly trembling, so much so that her cup clattered wildly on its saucer. She hastily placed her coffee on a small end table.

Van had said he loved her. *Loved* her. Lordy. And there was Alex, so big and handsome, brooding and scowling over her drawings. She realized suddenly that she was terrified of his reaction, and when he spoke she held her breath.

"It looks as though you've been working on this project

for months," he said. He bent his dark head and examined the sketches more closely. "They're good. Really good."

Her heart gave a little flip as his hands smoothed the paper. He had wonderful hands—long, sculptured fingers and broad, strong palms, hands like those of Michelangelo's *David*. Erin stared at them, mesmerized.

"Interesting the way you've tied in the terraces with those stone outcroppings. Are you worried about their being end-heavy?"

"I've designed those parapets at the end to act as truss beams. They'll carry the floor slabs." She had worried over that aspect of the plan and had had a consultant's help to calculate the figures.

"What's all this going to cost?" When Alex looked at her, his eyes once again drained her strength completely, and she had to fortify herself with the thought of his many women.

"I haven't yet written up the program or made any calls for estimates. I was in such a hurry to get this down."

"She has carte blanche, Alex," said Van. "It will be well worth whatever it costs."

She looked at Van, surprised. She hadn't heard *that* before.

"Okay, but I still say leave the waterfall out of it."

"No! Otter Run is an essential part of my design, and I have *no* intention of changing it."

Their eyes met and sparred defiantly.

"Now, Alex, you said if she could give you the answers—"

"Hold your horses, Van. I said I'd do it, and I'll do it. If I didn't, some fly-by-night outfit would milk you for all you're worth. There's no one else around who could do a good job on such a crazy proposal."

It was clear that he was exasperated at both of them.

When Erin glared at him, pointing out that Roberto Strata could, Alex silenced her with a black look.

"Then I should just let Bob Strata do it," he growled.

"Now, now." Van's hands went up in a placating gesture. Erin decided that Cecile really had her father wrapped around her little finger. It was the only reason she could imagine why Nicholas van Rijn would tolerate Alex Butler's irritating, giant ego.

Peace descended then and Erin watched silently as the tall, dark builder shook Van's hand in a pledge to build the house she'd designed. He would like to begin in early May, he said, if he could have the program and specs by then. His questioning eyes wilted her once more, but she gathered her strength and answered, "Yes, they'll be ready."

"Superb. What a lark this is going to be," Van exclaimed, and Erin heard Alex's disgruntled snort. "I'm having a party tomorrow night. We can celebrate the building of . . ." He was glowing magnanimously. "The house needs a name. What shall we call it?"

"You should name it, Van," Erin said.

Alex, she saw, had had enough of them both. His hand was already on the doorknob, and naming the place was just extra foolishness to him. She, too, was eager to be gone, eager to get back to her office and do something other than think about what lay ahead of her with these two men.

"No, Erin, you shall name it," Van said. "I insist."

She knew her cheeks were coloring; Nicholas van Rijn was certainly unlike her other clients.

"Well, I have to admit I already think of it as Whitewater."

"*Perfect*. Whitewater it shall be," he declared.

"Well, thank you, Van. I'm honored to name it. But now I really must go."

"I, too." Alex opened the door.

"*Wait*. Both of you. Come by tomorrow night. I want

people to meet the architect and the builder of White-water. Erin, bring Deirdre. I want to make that lovely lady's acquaintance again.'' That led to several minutes of conversation about Deirdre, and when Erin finally said good-bye, Alex was nowhere in sight. His irritation had no doubt got the better of him.

It was a difficult drive, the five minutes or so between Oakland and Shadyside; she found it hard to keep her mind on the traffic and pedestrians. She drove past the Cathedral of Learning and Mellon Institute without seeing them; her mind was still on the conversation in Van's office.

She felt torn between jubilation at having the chance to design Whitewater—and worry. Worry that bordered almost on panic. Now that she was actually committed, she wondered just how she was going to go through with it. How was she going to cope with Van's newly declared and undisguised love? And how was she going to cope with a domineering builder like Alex?

Stop it, Erin Kelly, she thought. Don't be as negative about Alex as he is about Whitewater. Think of the challenge. But she feared the greatest challenge wouldn't be fighting Alex's domination, it would be fighting her desire for him.

Deirdre had other plans and couldn't go to the party, much to her own and Erin's regret. Erin wanted her sister to meet Van again, and the sooner, the better. As it was, however, Van hadn't the time to moon over her at the party. There must have been a hundred people at his penthouse in the Allegheny Tower; wall-to-wall people sipping imported wine, nibbling crispy little canapés, and sampling various hot dishes, salads, rolls and desserts.

Erin decided it was a wonderful party. She met some interesting people, ate to her heart's content, and knew she looked her best. She had worn a long gray wool skirt with a black silk shirt that set off her auburn curls and her hair was behaving once more. She could safely say she looked sophisticated, and she was actually enjoying the feeling.

Mirrors in the room produced a myriad of reflections which showed that she was glowing and bright-eyed. The small jet earrings and delicate jet necklace she wore provided a nice contrast to her white skin. Obviously, it was therapeutic to be cosseted and admired. Van had told everyone who and what she was: Erin Kelly of Earth Architecture, the designer of his future summer home, Whitewater.

She saw Alex the minute he arrived, and not only was he the tallest, best-looking man there, but he was also the best dressed. He wasn't dapper—too many of the men there looked like male models—but he looked casually elegant in gray slacks and a burgundy cashmere turtleneck under a navy blazer.

Her eyes caught her reflection in a mirror again. There was a flush in her cheeks, her eyes were brighter than ever, and her lips, soft and moist. She felt her body prickling with excitement, but she took a deep breath and gave her full attention to the small knot of people clustered about her.

"Does your Earth Architecture follow any of the primitive American architectures?" asked a serious-faced young woman with a blond Afro. "You know—the Incan or Aztec style?"

Erin looked at her, pleased. "Why, yes, the South American Indians were the creators of earth architecture. Just think of those vast mesas of stone, the pyramids planned like mountains . . ."

Cecile was beside Alex, Erin noted, and clinging to his arm like an adorable kitten. She was in a white strapless gown that had very little covering her back. How did it stay up when she was nearly popping out of it? Erin wondered.

"Then, if I understand correctly, this type of architecture is more free and flowing," said someone at her elbow.

"That's right. It frees space and . . ." Erin continued her discourse, but much of her attention was on Cecile as she laughed up into Alex's face. Worse, however, was his reaction. He was looking down at her as though he were dazed, hypnotized. Erin blinked, ashamed of the terrible jealousy overwhelming her.

". . . and it utilizes straight lines and streamlined, flat-plane effects . . ." She was barely aware of what she was saying.

Every time Cecile introduced Alex to someone, she clung a little tighter. Erin realized with a start that she wanted to slay them both—Van's gorgeous, spoiled daughter and the man Cecile had chosen to be her lover, fling, or whatever. The man Erin herself could have had if she'd wanted just a temporary affair.

". . . and, of course, the structures all have an inherent elegance and serenity because they embody the characteristics of the region they inhabit."

The girl with the blond Afro, it turned out, was looking for an architect to redo the old Shadyside house she had just bought. Erin agreed to take a look, but all she really wanted at that point was to get into Mighty Mouse and head home to sulk.

Alex had seen her, of course, but he'd made no effort to approach or even greet her. He merely nodded to her from across the room. Van had joined her by then and was proudly escorting her from group to group in the now-thinning crowd.

"Are you enjoying yourself, my dear?" His arm was curved snugly about her waist.

"It's a wonderful party. I've made some good contacts and gained at least five pounds."

"And in all the right places, I see." He gave her a possessive squeeze and she remembered Cecile's irritating words: the van Rijns always got what they wanted.

"It's getting late, Van. I really should say good night. Thanks again for a wonderful time."

"There will be many more, my dear. Tell Deirdre I'm sorry she couldn't attend." He kissed her hand and seemed reluctant to let it go.

"Oh, I will. She was terribly disappointed."

"I believe I'll escort you to your car so you'll be safe."

"You'll do no such thing," she declared. "The watchman will be there and the parking area is well lit. Please, stay with your guests." Erin was relieved when his attention was claimed by one of those guests.

Cecile was alone when Erin moved toward the foyer and claimed her coat. At least Alex was gone.

"Cecile, thank you. It was lovely, but I'm sorry we didn't get a chance to talk."

"Thank you for coming. I told Alex you two were the stars of the evening."

Erin smiled. "Maybe. Our one brief moment in the sun."

"But this is just the beginning. Our house will put Laurel on the map and put you in the news."

"Oh, come now."

"By the way, Step One has been accomplished."

Erin was tired, exhausted in fact; she looked at Cecile blankly.

"You know . . . Alex. Step One in my plan to get Alex." Cecile's blue eyes glittered with excitement. "He's comfortable with me now and has even asked me out. There's a road rally tomorrow and his partner canceled, so I volunteered."

For the life of her, Erin couldn't respond, and she knew that if she smiled, it would be a horrible grimace.

"A road rally," said Cecile, interpreting her lack of

response as ignorance, "is a sports car club event. Alex needs a partner to read the map, watch for landmarks, and give him moral support and comfort." Her seductive smile would have put Cleopatra to shame. "We'll have dinner afterward, of course, and take our time getting back. It's up around Chagrin Falls, that neat area south of Cleveland."

"Well, have fun." Erin managed a pat on Cecile's shoulder, but the knot was back in her stomach again. Cold and hard and expanding by the second. It spread to her throat and settled there.

"Oh, fear not, I will. Toodle-oo. Wish us luck. Wish *me* luck."

Erin nodded. "Toodle-oo."

To top the evening off, Mighty Mouse wouldn't start. Punishment, no doubt, for her lustful thoughts of Alex and her hateful reaction to Cecile's happiness. The girl was sweet, really, in a spoiled, adolescent kind of way, and it was wrong, Erin thought, to want to throttle her.

She pushed her foot down on the accelerator again and again, but Mighty Mouse just snorted, coughed once, but didn't start. You little beast, she thought. You're just like Carl—undependable. Suddenly her door was opened and Erin jumped, startled. "What—"

"Let me try," was all Alex said.

He had picked up Mighty Mouse's distress cry instantly, but hadn't cared a fig about her all evening long. *Men.*

Erin climbed out, awkward in her long skirt, and caught her heel in its hem, bumping her head on the doorframe. She emitted a muffled "*damn.*"

Alex silently got behind the wheel and turned the key, and once more the car put on a pitiful performance. Then he got out and looked under the hood, after producing a flashlight from his pocket. She heard him sigh.

"I really *hate* this car," she said. "Something's always going wrong."

"How often do you have it serviced?" His voice was dangerously quiet.

"Serviced?" The notion was foreign to her. Carl had always taken care of maintenance. "I have things done when they're necessary."

Slamming down the hood, he handed her the key, and shook his head. "Better lock up, Ms. Kelly. It needs more than I can provide. Give Lafferty's a call tomorrow morning. They're on the next block. It's Sunday, but tell them you know me." His voice dripped disapproval. "I'll get you home—it's on my way."

Again, she thought, hating herself and him at that moment.

Erin followed him through the garage to where a little gray bullet stood gleaming under the overhead lights. She stared at it. It was a Saab just like hers, but this one was a healthy, well-fed cat in comparison with her own scraggly, unkempt Mouse. Worse, it looked exactly as her Saab had the day she'd chosen it. Sleek, powerful-looking, and just waiting to spring forward and eat up the highways.

Alex helped her in and she sank down into the passenger seat, which was covered with a thick, luxurious sheepskin.

"No wonder you care about my car," she murmured, feeling more miserable than ever as the old, familiar memories flooded over her. Harsh memories of a love gone sour. She pushed them away. She'd fly out of her skin if she had one more thing to worry about tonight.

As Alex's car purred up Forbes Avenue, past Pitt and the Carnegie Institute, she finally began to relax a bit and enjoy the way Alex handled the Saab. It was as though car and man knew each other intimately and made each other happy.

"You look beautiful tonight," he said unexpectedly.

"I do?" A warm swell of pleasure washed over her.

"Yes," he said rather gruffly.

"Thank you."

When he said nothing further, Erin cast about for a topic of conversation. It was too uncomfortable just sitting there in the dark, aware of his nearness.

"Maybe now you can tell me," she began lightly, "why you agreed to build the house. I can't actually believe you'd care all that much if someone else botched the job."

He looked at her and Erin saw his eyes flash in the light of an oncoming car. "I don't like to see anything messed up by incompetence."

"But you said earlier you wouldn't do it, and I know you don't want to work with me."

She wanted Alex to deny her statement, wanted him to say he took the job because he *did* want to work with her. Then she told herself to stop. They had shared a kiss up at Laurel but that meant nothing to a man who moved easily from woman to woman. His lips were probably sore from all the kissing he'd done, whereas she could count on the fingers of one hand how many men she had allowed to kiss her since her divorce.

"Van's in a position to throw a lot of work my way," he said finally. "Let's just say it's an exchange of favors. And as I said, I couldn't leave you two to the mercy of the wolves."

"I see." Erin's feelings were too tender, and she raged inside that that should be so. He didn't care about her— not in the least. He'd have jumped into her bed if she'd allowed him, but beyond that, there was nothing. Greed seemed to be his main reason for taking the damned job.

She felt the approach of hot, stinging tears behind her eyes, and a lump suddenly constricted her throat. As they sped along the winding road through Highland Park, she fought them back. She was appalled at the thought of crying in front of him.

Erin bit her lip and gulped a lot, but by the time they were crossing the Allegheny, the tears were rolling unchecked down her cheeks. She would not—damn it—use a tissue and call attention to her misery. She sniffed, then nearly strangled on the excess moisture pouring down the back of her throat.

"Okay, Kelly." He was irritated. "What is it? When I caught your eye back at Van's, I saw your dander was up, and now you're bawling. What have I done?"

"I'm *not* bawling," she said, and hiccuped.

"Oh, *hell*." He squirmed in his seat, then handed her a clean white handkerchief. "Here, keep it."

Erin needed to blow her nose, but she dabbed daintily at her eyes and nose instead, and wondered wildly what she could say. Alex was waiting for an answer to a question she couldn't answer truthfully.

"I know you're unhappy about my . . . my car," she began.

"Hey," he said, his hand reaching over and closing around hers, "if I'd thought it would do this to you . . ." He shook his head and gave her hand a comforting squeeze. "I'm sorry. It's none of my business what you do with your car."

"I . . . I ignore it on purpose." Her voice sounded small in the dimness.

Alex looked at her with curiosity. "Why would you do that?"

"It's a long story and it wouldn't interest you."

"Ah, but it would, Kelly—try me." For some reason she believed him.

"Well, maybe just a brief synopsis."

He nodded. "That would be fine."

Chapter Six

❧

Erin's fingers played nervously with the small beaded evening bag on her lap. "Well, my husband, or rather, my ex-husband, gave me the car. It was a gift. Sort of a symbol of a promise he made but never really intended to keep. The problem was that he liked women too much—all women." The tears were rolling again. "He was an architect, too, and he stole my work and passed it off as his own."

There was a long silence while she tried to collect herself. Alex expelled a long sigh. "Oh, boy," he said, "a nice guy."

"That's it. There's no more to tell except I loved him and I'm still resentful. It's been three years since I divorced him and I'm afraid of being hurt again the same way." Erin was strangely glad she was telling Alex all this.

"And while we're on the subject," she said, plunging on, "I was brooding about Carl when I made a fool of myself banging into your grader like that. Oh, Alex, I felt like such an idiot."

His profile was grim against the sudden flash of a streetlight as they passed it.

"I feel so ashamed to still be so bitter. I often wonder if I'll ever be the way I was before—"

"Why the hell shouldn't you feel bitter?" he snapped.

"And why add shame to your unhappiness?" The gruff words surprised her. It was almost as though he, too, knew about bitterness and hate and resentment.

They drove on in silence, the only noise the throaty growl of the Saab and the faint hiss of wind racing over its streamlined body.

"It seems to me that it's almost better not to marry," he said finally. "Not to get too close to anyone."

"Maybe," she whispered, wondering what terrible thing had happened to make him feel this way.

But he was right where the two of them were concerned. It was better not to get too close. All they ever seemed to do was argue, their stubborn wills pitted against each other. Then, too, there was Cecile, hell-bent on having him.

Erin put both hands to her cheeks in a sudden torment of confusion. Oh, God, it was so easy to love him; as easy as it was to be hurt and angered by him.

She pointed out Strawberry Way, then directed him to her dark farmhouse.

"You should have a light on in the house." He seemed concerned.

"I did. It must have burned out."

"And you should have outside lights. Someone could be waiting to jump you."

"Then maybe you should come in." She smiled in the darkness, pleased that he cared. "You can look under my bed and in all the closets while I make coffee. And I have a torte in the fridge."

"Homemade?"

"Of course."

She nearly exclaimed when she saw his limp had returned, but the grim set to his mouth warned her to keep silent. Erin filled the copper pot with water, measured out the coffee, and set the table with red place mats and pewter plates while Alex prowled around the house. To her surprise, he was serious about intruders.

She grinned when he returned. "Find anyone?"

"You need a German shepherd or a Doberman," he said glumly. "You're too isolated here."

His spirits weren't raised by the torte, the coffee, or the lively fire in the hearth.

"I've put you in a gloomy mood with my complaints about Carl," she said. "I'm sorry."

It was wonderfully strange having him here in her kitchen, eating her cake, with the firelight throwing enchanting shadows across his face and giving a bronze cast to his black hair. "You seemed so happy at the party."

"Did I?" His voice was dark.

"My goodness, I thought so. Cecile is so beautiful and is so . . . taken by you."

The sudden, shocking emptiness in his eyes was so tangible Erin could almost feel it. Her need to comfort him was so powerful that she reached across the small table and covered his hands with hers.

"It will be all right one of these days," she said quietly. "I know it will, Alex. It will be fine for both of us."

Having his big warm hands there beneath hers started such a fire in her she hurriedly withdrew them. Erin watched as a wry, disbelieving smile lifted one corner of his mouth. He was obviously touched by her small attempt to comfort him because his eyes had softened. Such fine, sensitive eyes . . .

"Erin Kelly, you're beautiful." He rose, came around the table, and drew her slowly to her feet. When he pulled her into his arms, Erin went so easily it was as though she belonged there.

His mouth was on hers before she could even think or protest, but she wouldn't have protested. Even with his words still in her thoughts, those words about not getting too close, she gave him her lips willingly.

As she was pressed hard against him and his warmth enfolded her, Erin's lips moved over his jaws and his cheeks, delighting in the masculine roughness of his skin. He smelled so good. She breathed in his wonderful scents: clean clothes, freshly scrubbed skin with the faintest hint of pine soap. Her grateful mouth soon sought his throat, the hollow at its base, and the broad expanse between his shoulders.

Alex's mouth did its own searching then, making a leisurely, sensual discovery of every inch of her face, teasing her fluttering lashes, skimming over the curves of her cheeks and chin, and using the tip of his tongue very gently at the corners of her lips.

A thrill plunged through her loins as his tongue met hers. When she didn't shut him out but allowed him to explore her mouth deeply and to press her body more closely to his own, she wondered if she meant to open the rest of herself to him . . .

It seemed to Erin that the sound he made then was a growl; a primitive, rasping noise from deep in his throat. His mouth, his arms, his whole body tensed and hardened as he claimed her. At that instant it was as though she were booty. Gone were his teasing, questing, gentle kisses and the slow, tantalizing discovery of her body.

He was hungry, terribly hungry, and Erin was carried along helplessly in the hot wave of his passion. At first she was startled by his ferocity, then inflamed by it, and finally she returned it.

His hands moved over her, hotly, urgently, first cradling her face and then spanning her throat with his thumbs as he stroked the creamy, smooth skin. Finally they moved over both her breasts, cupping them as though discovering their shapeliness and testing their heaviness.

Alex played with them then, a sensuous massage that made Erin gasp. Fire seemed to radiate through her body as his sensitive fingers kneaded and compressed her soft curves, pushing them together, then lifting and slowly rotating them, a breast filling each of his hands.

He lowered his head and soon there were two dark wet spots on her silk shirt where his hungry mouth had fastened to her erect nipples. She moaned, a strange, pleasurable sound, as he licked and nipped her, tempting, teasing . . .

As Alex began to unbutton her shirt the breath caught in her throat. She put a restraining hand on his. She had never meant to let things get so out of hand. Erin had been in such sweet ecstasy, with all her senses, all her awareness of him heightened and deepened, that the inevitable conclusion to such caresses had seemed distant.

Her eyes opened wide as reality took hold. Erin knew with every thinking part of her that she would be hurt by this man, but his hands had already opened her shirt and for the first time were moving over the silken skin of her naked breasts. He pulled her closer, his tongue plunging again and again into her suddenly resisting mouth.

She felt his sudden hardness between her legs when he grasped her small buttocks in both his hands and pulled her in and up against him. Her body had been open and vulnerable since he had dipped in and tasted her mouth's secrets. Now Erin was as hungry as he, melting against him, wanting that ultimate pleasure. Lord help her. She still felt fearful and hesitant, but her discipline and resolve were gone. Nothing mattered but this moment. She was in love with him, and come what may . . .

Soon her shirt was off and Alex's eyes were glittering over the lacy, black camisole next to her white skin.

"Sexy." His voice was husky as his hands slipped up beneath it, caressing her skin as they went. He cupped and lifted her breasts so they spilled out over the top of the flimsy lace. They thrust forward, full, pink-tipped, and pure white against the black silk.

He laughed, delighted, and when he gave her a little shake, she jiggled deliciously. Alex then bent his head and his mouth closed over one hard, puckered bud. A torrent of fire exploded deep within her, a torrent that rushed into Erin's bloodstream and reached every trembling part of her.

"Too many clothes," Alex whispered against her lips after he had removed her gray skirt and encountered a long slip and panty hose. Then she was naked, the air chilling the parts of her not warmed by his lips and his hands and his body.

Erin saw her beauty reflected in his appreciative dark eyes and felt a sudden, overwhelming tenderness. How wonderful that she could give him such pleasure. Who would have thought that grief would bring them together this way?

She had been standing almost like a statue, allowing him to gaze at her, melt her with his hands, and kiss her all over, but when he pulled away for a moment to remove his shirt, she saw his painful urgency. In his haste to undo his belt buckle, he was clumsy and impatient.

"Alex, let me."

While he continued to stroke and cover her soft body with kisses, Erin undressed him until all that remained of his clothing were his snug jockey shorts. Shorts that could barely contain his excitement.

When he stood before her, completely unclothed, she had only seconds to gaze at him, to run her hands over the crisp hair on his chest and along his body, before she was lifted into his arms.

"Where?" he asked, his voice hoarse. "Here? The sofa?"

"Upstairs . . . my bedroom," she gasped, laughing. Alex had already taken one pink nipple between his teeth and was biting it gently. She grabbed his head and squeezed it hard against her breasts, and the sight of his glossy black hair against her white skin sent a shudder of delight pulsing through her.

"Oh, Alex, please, let's go up right now."

He carried her up the stairs, brushing kisses over every part of her that his lips could reach.

"God, Erin—oh, God . . ." His voice was husky and she saw that his face was a tortured mask before he buried it once again between her breasts. She stroked his black hair, loving the way it felt beneath her fingers, loving the way he was murmuring her name over and over and pressing kisses on her body. And she loved the way he was holding her. Hungrily, yet almost reverently, as though she were a treasure he was about to possess.

Alex gently placed her on the bed and lay down beside her, and his tongue and lips were marking a moist trail from her mouth to the hard, dusky center of each peaked breast, on down over her rounded belly until he finally rested at the soft curve, that soft, dark shadow between her legs.

She opened herself to him willingly, and a small moan of pleasure parted her lips. Alex had found and was slowly tantalizing the more erotic areas of her body until there was no more time. She guided that hard, conquering part of him, to the velvety, moist part of her that was hungering for him and could wait no longer.

When they had become one wild, glad, and united thing, it was as though a tightly furled bud within her had opened into a hot, vibrant flow of sensations. Suddenly Erin was laughing and crying and covering Alex's face and chest with her grateful kisses. She had forgotten, completely forgotten, that it was heaven.

* * *

They slept in each other's arms until Alex woke her with a kiss. It was still dark.

"I have to leave, Erin. It's six o'clock and I have an appointment at eight." He was whispering, as though hesitant to waken her completely.

Erin turned on her bedside lamp and blinked at him, this man who now held her so firmly by the heart strings. He was already dressed.

"Do you always look this good at six in the morning?" Alex sat on the bed beside her, a wicked glint in his eyes as he gave her a long kiss. "Don't worry, I'm under control." He held up both his hands. "You're safe—at least for now."

"Do you know you're beautiful, Alex Butler?" When he scowled at her, she said, "Well, you *are*."

"Men aren't beautiful."

"Some men are," she insisted, stroking his unshaven face.

He gave her yet another sweet kiss, caressing her cheek and chin with his fingertips. "Kelly, let's remember last night when we do battle over Whitewater." His eyes flickered over her one last time, and then he was gone.

She was still in bed, naked, a sheet pulled up to cover herself, and she thought, how silly. Alex had seen all of her there was to see. Not only seen her, but tasted and known her as well. At that moment she couldn't imagine being angry at him or arguing with him ever again.

And Cecile, she thought lazily as she drifted off to sleep again, poor Cecile was still back at Step One.

When Erin finally woke up a few hours later, the sun was streaming through her bedroom window, spilling over her bed and warming her face.

She lay quietly, remembering Alex's lusty lovemaking and imagining him, tall and dark, stretched out beside her in the old four-poster bed. His hair was so black against the white pillow and one long arm had been flung outside the yellow-sprigged coverlet as he lay sleeping.

She stretched, savoring the delicious feeling. It felt so good to be a woman—a "ravished woman." A pixie smile curved her lips at the thought, and she lifted the covers above her so she could look down at her body, at the pale swells of her breasts, the small round of her belly, and her curvaceous thighs.

Her breathing quickened. Alex had practically devoured her last night, yet there wasn't a mark on her smooth skin to show for it. How had he managed to be such a fierce, almost primitive lover and be so gentle at the same time? Gentle and sensitive to her needs.

She rose finally to shower and pull on a pair of jeans and a deep green turtleneck sweater. Old, comfortable clothes. She stepped into her red fluffy slippers and padded down to the kitchen. It was ten o'clock on a Sunday morning, certainly time for her to be up and doing.

The kitchen took Erin completely by surprise. Everything was exactly as it was when Alex had carried her up the stairs last night. Pewter plates and empty cups were still on the table, and the chairs were askew. But, no, not *everything* was the same. Her clothing had been on the floor, right where it had fallen, and now it was carefully draped over a chair. She smiled. Oh, Alex . . .

Erin made fresh coffee and fixed herself an egg, bacon, and toast before calling Lafferty's about the Saab. She couldn't call Deirdre, who was vacationing in Florida, so she padded about some more, daydreaming, watering plants, washing up, feeling at loose ends.

There were any number of things she could do: shine her copper-bottomed pans, do laundry, write letters. Instead she drifted aimlessly from room to room before she realized she was waiting for something. Waiting for the telephone to ring.

Surely Alex would call her when he finished with his appointment. After last night, wouldn't he want to hear her voice as much as she wanted to hear his?

She had just poured a second cup of coffee and was looking out her window at the birds clustering and chirping around the bird feeder when it hit her. He wouldn't be calling at all. He was with Cecile. The two of them would be roaring along country roads all day and then have dinner together. An appointment, Alex had said. An eight o'clock appointment.

Of course he hadn't known Cecile had told her about the rally, and of course he wasn't going to leave her bed and then confess he was going off with another woman. Not even if it were something as innocent as a sports car event.

But was it? She remembered Cecile's sultry smile the night before, and how marvelous she had looked in white. How she had clung to Alex's arm and how he had appeared to be completely captivated.

Her coffee had grown cold. She poured it out, washed the cup, and decided it was a good time after all to do the chores she usually avoided. Anything was better than such negative thoughts. She got out the copper cleaner and a sponge, and took down her big frying pan from the pegboard. She would start with the hardest first.

The next day, Monday, Erin took two buses to Shadyside, and her day was filled from the beginning: phone calls and a meeting with the first of the many specialists she would be consulting in connection with Whitewater. The structural, mechanical, electrical, and acoustical engineers.

She knew Alex must have tried to call her office during the day, but her phone was tied up so much of the time, and he himself was so busy, it was no wonder she didn't

hear from him. Erin made a good start at the program,
the report that would clearly spell out everything
involved in the building of Whitewater—all the costs,
construction methods, materials, schedules, and
deadlines.

The day had been very productive, but it was still nice
to get home to her nest. Erin popped a small crab and rice
casserole into the oven and began to make a salad.

Alex would probably call this evening, or she would call
him. Maybe he would even stop by. There was an apple pie
in the freezer, she remembered. There was nothing but one
lone apple pie, but that wouldn't be his reason for coming.

When the telephone rang, she flew to it with bits of let-
tuce and spinach still clinging to her wet hands.

"Hello." Her legs were wobbly.

"How are you, my dear? This is Van."

"Oh. Hello, Van." Her voice sounded strange, a voice
with no animation.

"Is everything all right? You sound far away."

"I'm fine."

Was this the way she was going to be from now on?
Waiting for the phone to ring and being devastated when
it wasn't Alex? Her heart sank. She didn't want that kind
of life.

"The reason I'm calling," Van went on, "is to invite
you to a grand soirée tonight."

"Well, Van, I thought I'd stay in tonight." She peered
out her kitchen window at the darkening horizon and could
see that the wind was picking up; treetops were waving
about and there was an angry flurry of snow in the air.
"I've had a really busy day—"

"My dear child, this isn't just *any* party. Cornelius
Scanlon will be there. The Cornelius Scanlon of the bank-
ing Scanlons, and he's thinking of building a home in West
Virginia. A mountain home. Erin, this is a must for you."

She went to her rocker, trailing the long telephone cord behind her, and plopped into it. Van was right. It *was* a must.

"Thank you for asking me. I guess I *should* go. What time?"

"I'll send the car for you at eight-thirty. We can make our entrance around nine. Erin, I want it to be a grand entrance—I want Punch Scanlon to be impressed by you in every way."

"I'm not sure I can manage that."

"Wear that dress you wore to White Bark." It was practically a command, and before Erin could say another word, Van said good-bye and hung up.

She clapped the phone sharply into its cradle and went back to her salad making. What that all boiled down to was the fact that Punch Scanlon was likely to be more impressed by her body than by her work.

Brooding while she ate, Erin wondered why Alex didn't call. But there was still lots of time. He was probably at the Shawcrest site . . . or out of town again, for all she knew. When one had a helicopter, traveling was simple.

She finished dinner, washed the dishes, and continued scouring the copper pans she had begun the day before—scoured them with a vengeance. She was ready to admit by now that she was uneasy. Why in the world hadn't he called? Was he ill? Had his leg gotten worse, and had he perhaps fallen down his stairs?

She dried her hands, quickly found his number, and dialed. When there was no answer, she didn't know what to think. It was all so strange. She was beginning to feel as though their night together had been a dream.

Erin saw that it was already eight o'clock. Van's chauffeur would arrive in half an hour, so she dressed hurriedly, and not in the dress Van had requested. Instead she pulled on a long rust-and-cream plaid skirt and a cream-colored turtleneck top. It was rebellion, pure and simple; she couldn't care less if Cornelius "Punch" Scanlon was impressed with her looks or not.

As it was, the big man never came. She and Van milled about with fifty other people making small talk, and Erin wished she were home. She was worried sick about Alex. Either something terrible had happened to him or . . . She bit down on her lower lip and could hardly bear to think about the alternative. She could hardly believe that he had taken what he wanted and was no longer interested in her. Good God, but she had been easy. And he didn't want an involvement; he had made that clear.

"Van, I'm tired. I'd really like to go home," she said finally. "I'll meet Mr. Scanlon another time."

"Just another fifteen minutes," her escort coaxed, and then his voice brightened. "Ah, here's Cecile. And Alex. Well, well, I had no idea they were coming. I only knew that dinner was on their agenda."

Van took Erin's arm and she felt herself being propelled toward the newcomers. For some time she neither heard, felt, nor saw anything. She was deep within herself, swept down into a numb darkness.

"Hello, you two. How was dinner?" Van kissed his daughter on the cheek.

"We went to the most marvelous little Syrian place in Bloomfield." Cecile was sparkling. "It's in an old house on the second floor and their baba ghanoush is heavenly. And their baklava . . ." She kissed her fingers. "Daddy, you really must take Erin sometime."

Alex nodded at them and thrust his hands deep into his pockets. "Good evening." It was a baritone murmur.

The men exchanged pleasantries and Cecile added an animated comment or two, but for the life of her, Erin couldn't have said what they talked about. Her wide, unwavering eyes were on Alex, daring him to look at her, to explain what he was doing with Cecile and why he was acting as though nothing had happened between them.

"Ooh, it looks like a fun party." Cecile was bubbling. "*Look*. A combo just arrived. Oh, Alex, will you dance with me? Say you will."

He briefly touched her happy face. "Sure, but just for a little—"

"And there are the Harpers. I thought they were still in Gstaad." Cecile waved wildly and grabbed Alex's arm. "Come on, you gorgeous hunk, I want you to meet some of my friends. Ta-ta, you two. Have fun." She gave Erin a meaningful look.

"Ms. Kelly." Alex's thickly lashed eyes met hers before he moved off with Cecile. "I assume you've begun the program?"

Ms. Kelly, she thought in aching bewilderment. Erin wanted to cry out and demand to know what was wrong. Dear Lord, this wasn't the man who had given her the most rapturous night she'd ever experienced. This man was a stranger.

"I've made a good beginning," she answered in a small, stiff voice as Van's arm circled her waist. She welcomed the gesture and gave him a tremulous smile. Dear Van. It seemed that she may have given her heart to the wrong man. Erin Kelly, you poor fool . . .

Erin tossed in her bed all night, and by early morning she had decided she would confront Alex. If he thought he could treat her any shabby way his heart desired and get off without any sort of explanation, he had another think coming.

It was nine A.M. when Erin drove Mighty Mouse up the bumpy land to Alex's mall. She slipped into her construction boots, got out of the car, and slammed the door. Of course it would be just her luck that he wasn't here.

An unexpected deep voice made her jump. "Well, Ms. Kelly." He was suddenly behind her and his eyes seemed to be smoldering with anger. "What brings you to a project that makes you see red?"

It was cruel of him. Alex knew she'd been embarrassed by her rash words and had apologized for them. All she could do for several long, terrible moments was breathe and stare at him.

"Why do you *suppose* I'm here?" she said finally.

He didn't answer. His stormy eyes swept over her plaid skirt, leather blazer, and ridiculous clunky boots, and she was outraged.

"If I were a man, Alex Butler, I'd mop up the floor with you. Pretending to care just to get me into bed." She nearly choked on the last word.

"I was going to call you today. Construction starts in early May, so give yourself plenty of time to make any changes my engineers may want." It seemed he hadn't heard a word she'd said.

Her eyes widened. Erin could almost feel sparks shooting from them as she realized he meant to ignore the issue. But something wasn't right. His own eyes didn't match the cutting words he'd just spoken. She softened, uncertain.

"Alex, what in the world is it? What's *happened?*"

"Let's just stick to business, shall we?" His eyes were distant now, seeming to pull away from her.

Erin took a deep, shaky breath. She had come for a blistering showdown, fully intending to let him know he was dealing with a force, but now . . .

She controlled her voice and her words carefully. "Alex, I came here to talk to you because I . . . wanted things to be right between us. I cared. And you know what? I've just discovered that if this is the kind of person you are, I don't *want* anything between us."

Chapter Seven

In the days that followed, Erin went all out to complete the blueprints and the specs for Whitewater. She was grateful that her professional detachment allowed her to work efficiently, to meet for consultations, and even to speak with Alex on the telephone.

As she listened to his distant, businesslike voice speaking about estimates, materials, and the techniques he would use, she realized what a terrible mistake she had made. There wasn't the slightest indication that he treasured the night they had spent together. How *could* she have done such a stupid thing? She hadn't left Chicago and friends she loved to come here and start another heartbreak all over again.

When she delivered the completed program to Alex in Van's office, they were like two strangers. Erin was reserved and Alex was a cold, distant man whose dark eyes were stony when they happened to meet hers. His lips were tightly clamped together when he wasn't speaking.

She stared at the small muscle jumping deep in his jaw, and was chilled. Would she ever know why Alex was so angry with her that he should grit his teeth?

The next time she saw him, construction had already begun. It was a lovely spring day late in May when Van took her to the site in his company helicopter.

Erin had eyes only for the construction. She simply couldn't believe all that had been accomplished since she'd last been there. The stone footings were already in place, those platforms from which the bolsters supporting the two terraces and the bedroom wing spanning Otter Run would rise, and everything was progressing on schedule. No, ahead of schedule. Even the weather was cooperating. As Alex walked toward them Erin felt herself tense.

"Well, well," said Van. "Progress has been made."

Alex laughed. "I should hope so." After his first polite greeting to Erin, he ignored her.

"The footings look wider than I had anticipated," Van said.

"That's because Mr. Butler felt three feet would be better than the two feet I had originally wanted," Erin interjected coolly. "He's still extremely concerned about flooding."

Alex's eyes swept over her, as stony as ever, and she wanted to kick him. She couldn't abide a man who refused to communicate.

Van exclaimed suddenly, "Is that Cecile I see down by the lake?"

"She came up with me." Alex's voice was muffled as he bent to look at something.

It gave Erin a sharp twinge to see his black hair escaping beneath the hard hat and curving over the collar of his jacket; hair as black and gleaming as a crow's wing. Her fingers had smoothed it and her mouth had caressed it, and the very thought made her bite down hard on her lip. If it took pain to take her mind off such memories, so be it.

Van stretched his hand out toward her. "My sweet, let's go down. I see Cecile has something to show us."

Cecile was waving at them.

"You go ahead, Van. I have something to discuss with Mr. Butler." Alex had been so cold and downright rude she couldn't contain her anger another minute.

"Very well, my dear. I think perhaps Cecile has found

the stretch where we can put the beach. I intend to put down some white sand.''

Erin watched as Van carefully navigated the uneven path down toward the lake, then she turned to Alex. A fine trembling had already tensed her body and she crossed her arms tightly, squeezing them against her breasts.

''All right, Alex.'' Her voice was low and she struggled to keep a quiver out of it. ''Enough's enough—I think I deserve to know what's wrong.''

His mouth tilted sardonically at one corner. ''What would be wrong, Kelly? Hell, everything's dandy.'' There was a mutinous look on his face.

If only she could remember him as he was now, nasty, sarcastic, and completely unreasonable. But Erin knew her memories of their lovemaking would win out instead.

''Damn it, Alex, why are you so angry with me?'' She felt small and fragile and very breakable. Her eyes were huge with bewilderment, like pools of turquoise against her pale skin as she stared at him, waiting. She saw that small movement deep inside his jaw. He was gritting his teeth again and it was clear he was disgusted with her. ''It's just not fair,'' she cried. ''You *have* to tell me what's wrong.''

His fingers were suddenly biting into her arms.

''*Alex.*''

She had only a glimpse of the grim lines around his mouth before it captured hers, and the kiss he gave her was so painful it brought tears to her eyes. When he finally released her, her voice shook.

''I hope you feel better, now that you've punished me sufficiently.'' She felt as though he had struck her.

''*Punished* you?''

''It seems clear enough,'' she gasped.

Cecile came up over the hill then, and Alex was scowling at Erin's bruised and swollen mouth and at the way she was rubbing her throbbing arms. They ached, she thought, clear down to the bones.

"Hi, people." The look Cecile gave Erin was far from happy.

"Hello, Cecile." Erin turned away from the girl's glacial blue eyes and toward the footings. "Yes, I think they're quite satisfactory," she managed to say to Alex, hating her attempt at pretense and hating both of them even more.

"Well, I have interesting news," Cecile said. "Daddy is leaving for Texas on Tuesday. He's not sure how long he'll be gone, and he's appointed me his representative here at the site."

As Erin stared at her Cecile's face assumed a look of triumph. Step Two would soon be accomplished, she seemed to be saying—frequent togetherness with Alex Butler.

Alex smiled and gently chucked her under the chin. "Well, honey, don't be surprised if you get bored. Excuse me, I want to see Van." He strode off without another look in Erin's direction.

Well, if Cecile wanted the likes of him, Erin thought miserably, she could jolly well have him. He had seen how hurt she was and he didn't care, and that kiss . . . She turned from Cecile blindly, knowing the kiss had been punishment, whether Alex realized it or not.

"Just a minute, *Mrs. Kelly.*" Despite the numbness creeping over her, Erin's dander rose at Cecile's imperious tone of voice.

"Yes?" Her eyes held a quiet warning but Cecile was undeterred.

"Stay away from Alex." The words were expelled in a low, explosive whisper, like a lashing whip. "Isn't one man enough for you?"

Erin stared at her, uncomprehending, thinking that the visit to the site had been a nightmare.

"Oh, don't look so innocent and proper." Cecile was furious, as furious as Alex had been.

"Cecile, I can't imagine what this is all about." She was growing more upset by the instant and afraid the men would hear.

"Oh, come *on*. My father's wild about you—that's what it's all about. You're stringing Daddy along and you're trying to make Alex Butler on the side. I've seen how you look at him, and after the nasty way you treated him. Not wanting him . . ."

Erin saw then that Cecile's eyes were bright with unshed tears.

"Don't try to wriggle out of it. You have the hots for Alex—even after I told you he was mine. I love my father, Erin. I won't stand by and let you wrap him around your little finger while you act all sweet and loving without meaning it."

Erin had all she could do to maintain an outward appearance of normalcy as Van joined them. Cecile, on the other hand, was like a chameleon. She was cool and poised as she walked them part way up the widened dirt path to the helicopter landing. Her gracious farewell was a marvel, as though she'd just served them tea in her manor house.

What a frightful tangle, Erin thought as Van's pilot directed the chopper skyward. Van wanted to hold her hand and she didn't object. It was a comfort somehow—but Lord, what a tangle.

Erin's long, unhappy sigh went unheard as she brooded over her encounters with both Cecile and Alex. It just served to show that things should be kept on a strictly professional basis between architect and client and builder. Nothing but business. She sighed again and gently withdrew her hand from Van's warm clasp.

Erin was thankful that her problem was at least temporarily

solved while Van was in Texas. She was thankful, too, that the progress of Whitewater was unaffected by the coolness between its builder and its architect.

When she drove up to the site in early June, Cecile greeted her cordially, just as though their last meeting hadn't been an angry one. It was a relief, really, and Erin felt in command of the situation and of herself. She walked about, eagerly examining the progress that had been made.

"It looks fine," she declared. "I'm pleased."

"I hoped you would be." Cecile looked mollified. "Alex is good, no matter what you may think." She started to move off. "Sorry I can't chat, but there's a call waiting for me."

"Cecile, about Alex"—Erin raised her voice—"that's way in the past. I know his work is good."

Alex, moving like a panther, came up behind her just then. He surely had heard her comment but pretended otherwise.

"Hello, Kelly." The deep resonance of his voice struck a painful memory.

"Hello, Alex." She had wondered how she'd be when she faced him again. Now she decided she was doing very well indeed, at least on the outside.

"The walls are beautiful." She indicated the three-foot-thick mass of concrete that constituted Whitewater's foundation.

He gave a dry laugh. " 'Beautiful' is hardly the word I'd use, but if you say so."

For just an instant there was a familiar glimmer of amusement in his deep brown eyes, and she had to take hold of herself. She wondered if they were both remembering the same thing—the time when she had said *he* was beautiful.

She looked back quickly toward the safety of the walls.

"Kelly, I'm sorry I hurt you the last time you were here. I certainly didn't mean to bruise you."

"You didn't." She was embarrassed. "It's . . . all right."

There was an awkward silence until he put his dark hand on the concrete and patted it.

"I hope to hell this holds up under the stress."

It was the very thing she needed. "I thought we both agreed"—she bit off the words—"along with your engineers, I might add, that keying the foundation into that rock ledge on the southwest would solve any problems."

He shrugged. "There are always unforeseen circumstances."

She held her tongue and changed the subject. "And things are going smoothly otherwise? No delays on any of the materials?"

He shook his head. "Cecile's been a miracle worker. She's damned good with the tradesmen and suppliers."

"Well, well," said Erin.

"Best thing Van could have done, getting Cecile up here."

"Yes. Well . . ."

Erin wanted to cry on her way back to Glenshaw, but remembering what had happened after her last bout of tears while driving, she held off. When she got home, she let loose and discovered, surprisingly enough, that it was not Cecile with whom she was angry. It was Alex.

He called her from time to time; always at the office, always concerning business, and always brief and to the point. She came to expect nothing more.

By the time Erin made her second visit to Laurel during Van's absence, she was tougher, accepting Alex's betrayal as a lesson learned. She no longer pined away for him, but he had best tread carefully, she thought darkly. She was a sleeping lioness and would never forget he had used her and then casually thrown her away.

As she neared Laurel Lake Erin vowed she would be pleasant but professional with him—the way she meant to be with Van when he returned. But never again would she make the mistake she had made on this project. *Never*.

When she spied Cecile at the site, Erin decided that, remarkably, this was the first time that she herself was dressed more attractively. Perhaps it was an omen of better things to come. Cecile was mucking about in muddy green deck shoes and a dreadful yellow-and-pink denim slack outfit that made her look like a floozy.

"Hello, Cecile." Erin smiled at the younger woman.

"Hello, there. We haven't seen you for a while."

Cecile's eyes swept over her in a look of such grudging admiration that Erin was tickled. She didn't pay all that much attention to clothes, but today she had lucked out in cotton knit shorts and a matching top. The shorts were perfectly sensible, but they did show off her long legs, and the top was a sleeveless, V-neck pullover. Both were turquoise and emphasized not only the unusual color of her eyes but her abundant curves.

Alex's men momentarily stopped their work and stared at her. Someone whistled. Erin went calmly about her inspection.

The form work, she saw, was under way for the first-floor slab, the slab that would eventually extend into one of the cantilevered terraces. She was poking around, giving it a thorough examination, when Alex strode up.

"Hello, Kelly."

"Good morning, Alex," His eyes took in her bare legs and her little sleeveless top, and seemed to see beyond it, to the soft swells it hid. "I finally made it," she said with the friendly reserve she had vowed to achieve. "Things have really been hectic around my office."

He nodded, his eyes continuing to move over her face and body. A brooding expression touched his face, as though he were painfully aware of her femininity.

What right had he to look at her like that? She thought, suddenly bitter. Undressing her with his eyes and making it perfectly clear that he remembered. In those few seconds she, too, was remembering their lovemaking all over again, and felt hurt and furious all over again—and eager to hurt him.

"I'd like to know when you'll be pouring the slab for the first floor." Her words were so sharp it was a pity she had looked at his mouth.

He blinked, as though suddenly released from a reverie. "I can't tell you the exact hour. Why? Does it matter?"

"I just want to be here."

"And why would that be?"

She caught his eyes on her mouth just then and felt resentment rushing through her veins, resentment at her body's violent response to him. She had been so sure her recovery was nearly complete . . .

"I don't want it poured at true level," she snapped. "The cantilever—"

His narrowed eyes stopped her. "Do you think I don't know an elementary thing like that?"

She held her ground. "You might not be here, and your field superintendent doesn't exactly fill me with confidence."

"*I'll* be here," he said emphatically. "Now, is there anything else?"

"I suppose the reinforcement bars will arrive in time?" She wished she could think of something important to complain about.

"Of *course*," Cecile chimed in, having just returned from her telephone call. "They wouldn't dare fail to deliver. They're scheduled to arrive two weeks from now.''

"If that's all, " Alex said crisply, "I'll get back to work.''

"That's all for now, but I do want to be informed of the pouring.'' Her words were like little icicles snapping off.

Cecile looked at her with a certain respect as Alex stalked off. "You would've made a good drill sergeant,'' she said.

Erin burst out laughing; she couldn't help it. Cecile seemed to have the knack, accidentally or on purpose, of saying the wrong thing and popping up at the wrong time.

A sudden, deafening racket surprised them all and set Cecile to waving excitedly when she saw the helicopter approaching.

"*Oh*,'' she cried, "it's *Daddy*.''

The master of Whitewater was home from his Texas travels, it seemed, and was paying a call.

Erin hung back as Van embraced his daughter and shook Alex's hand. Looking trim and tanned, he was immaculately dressed as a country gentleman. Erin wondered if he ever had a hair out of place.

Van's eyes went to her finally, and she realized by his eager look that he was saving her for "dessert.'' She couldn't avoid his eager embrace, not without embarrassing or offending him, but it was his kiss that shocked her—a long, hard kiss on the lips. A hungry kiss, for the first time.

Then he was standing between "his girls,'' smiling down at them, proudly possessive. Erin's own smile was sheepish; this was hardly the professional relationship she had planned to initiate upon his return.

She looked at Alex. The black, disapproving look on his face revealed that he had witnessed Van's kiss. Good! she thought. He didn't want her, so it was rather nice that he saw another man did. She would just disentangle herself from Van another time, but it should be very soon.

After the reunion Van was shown the progress that had been made, then he dispatched his pilot. He would return to Glenshaw with Erin, he declared, and instructed the pilot to pick him up in her backyard at precisely five-thirty.

She wanted to laugh wildly at the insanity of it all. Since Erin had moved to that quiet rural area, choppers had been buzzing about like gnats on a summer's day and chauffeured cars kept coming and going. What must the neighbors think?

Van looked at his watch. "Erin, if we leave right now, we'll arrive close to five-thirty. The ride will give us time to catch up."

As he took her arm and led her to the Saab, Erin felt that same wild silliness bubbling up, ready to spill over. Van, it seemed, had no idea that Mighty Mouse was such a trial, that it might or might not get him to Glenshaw on time. But she had been treating the car better. She'd actually had it serviced, and it seemed to be behaving itself.

Van insisted on driving and she sighed with relief when the little beast started. It putted loudly down to the highway and then zoomed along, full of vigor, as in the old days.

"Well, my dear, Whitewater is actually beginning to look something like a house. I'm pleased."

"I'm glad. Things have gone well and so fast. It's been such a dry spring, and that's made it easier. I suppose we're due for a deluge."

She waited for him to go on, with questions about the construction, perhaps, but instead he said, "Yes. But now tell me, what about you and Alex?" He shot a probing glance at her.

"What do you mean?"

"Have you developed the rapport you felt was so necessary?"

She didn't realize she'd been holding her breath. "I'm afraid not. We . . . tolerate each other."

"Ah. A pity. Cecile says she's noticed a certain coolness between you, and that she has tried to smooth things over."

Erin gave a delicate snort.

"What was that?" Van cocked his head toward her.

"I didn't say anything."

"Well, my dear, don't worry your pretty head over Butler. When the house is finished, you needn't see him again. The fellow is fine as a builder, but one wouldn't want him as a friend, I suspect. No taste or sensitivity worth mentioning."

Erin stared numbly out the window at the Pennsylvania countryside passing by: rolling, forested hills, farms with cattle and sheep and goats, ponds with ducks, green corn standing almost knee high. All so beautiful. She had had such wonderful hopes that she would be happy once she was home again . . .

"I suppose you're right," she said finally. Memories of Alex's passionate but sensitive lovemaking made her feel like a traitor, but when she remembered everything else, she felt justified in agreeing with Van. God, she had a headache.

The headache wasn't helped any by Van. He'd barely said ten words about the house and she fidgeted while he went on and on about his business, the new company he'd acquired, and the superb food he had eaten in Texas. By the time he turned Mighty Mouse into her long driveway, Erin's head felt too big for her skin and there was a painful throbbing behind her eyes. She was relieved that his helicopter was waiting.

"Well, my dear, I do like the house. I'm more than satisfied. Whitewater will be a jolly little place. I'll be in touch . . ." He gave her cheek a pat and strode toward his helicopter.

She didn't wait for the bird to take off, and it was a good thing. She wanted to heave a rock at it. "Jolly little place," indeed.

Once inside, Erin swallowed two aspirin and put the kettle on for tea. She wanted to forget Alex and Van. Both of them were nothing but trouble.

She kicked off her shoes, went about opening some windows, and decided that she was hungry. A grilled-cheese sandwich would be nice with the tea. And pickles. Homemade bread-and-butter pickles from the best pickle recipe in the world—her mother's.

Feeling infinitely sad but finally pain free, Erin took the sandwich, pickles, and tea to her drafting board. She loaded the food onto a stool at her side, turned on the adjustable lamp, and stared at the pencil sketch before her: a straight-on perspective of Whitewater.

Nothing mattered to her now but the house. Her poor house. Alex didn't give a damn about it—he was only building it in exchange for favors. It wouldn't surprise her a bit if he hoped a major storm would sweep the whole thing downstream and into the lake. And Van—Van obviously didn't give a damn, either.

She munched half a jar of the delicate, paper-thin pickles and onion slices while she brooded over her sketch. Whitewater was going to be a wonderful place, if she did say so herself—and who would if she didn't!

The site had completely determined the features and character of the house. It seemed to leap out of the forest behind it; a perfect blending of shelter and nature. Beautiful in every season. She decided that Frank Lloyd Wright would have been proud of her . . .

Erin sniffed, dabbing at her damp eyes with her fingers. She felt wonderfully maudlin and finally went off to bed early, intoxicated by two aspirin, half a jar of pickles, and the wonderful prospect of a completed Whitewater.

Chapter Eight

Things fell into a pattern with Van home. When he insisted they visit the site twice a week during July and early August, an easy trip with his helicopter, Erin went without protest despite her other projects. This house had become her baby, something on which she could focus her lonely thoughts and much of her attention.

She and Van were at Whitewater the morning the second-floor slab was poured; it was a cause for jubilation. Cecile, who had stayed on as her father's representative after his return, was lifted off her feet by Alex for a hearty smack on the cheek. Van gave Erin a hug and a kiss, another kiss on the mouth.

It was all right, Erin thought defensively. Van had been as tame as a pussy cat since his return from Texas, after that hearty kiss Alex had witnessed. So tame, in fact, that she hadn't needed to say a word to him about their relationship becoming more professional.

Now she saw another of Alex's black looks directed at them, and it seemed a direct reaction to Van's kiss. Erin bristled. It was almost as if he didn't want Van near her. He didn't want her himself, but he didn't want anyone else to have her, either. She'd just about had it with Alexander King Butler.

She bided her time and when Van and Cecile clambered happily down to the lake to take measurements for a dock,

Erin picked her way over to where Alex was checking some materials.

"Alex . . ."

His dark, winged brows met in a scowl as he turned toward her. It was such an unfriendly look that his words shocked her.

"Kelly, this is going to be one hell of a house. I hate to admit it, but I'm almost fond of it."

Erin felt a brief blossoming of pleasure before she snipped it off in the bud. "Thank you—that's very nice—but why do you hurl such hateful looks at us all the time?" Now that she had started, she knew it would be hard to stop.

"I'm being paid to build a house," he said, his voice low, "not to be popular. And I find it easy to be hateful under certain conditions."

"You certainly do." She was whispering so the nearby workmen wouldn't hear. "I've never known anyone quite as hateful." Here it comes, she thought—there was just no holding back her bitterness and resentment. "Making love to me and then ignoring me, just like an old shoe." She was surprised tears weren't flowing. "You used me, Alex. Do you know how that makes me feel?"

"That's right." His voice was dull, ugly in its dullness. "I used you. And it seems I used another man's property."

"What?" Erin's eyes were suddenly moist, a shimmering blue-green in her blanched face. "What did you say?"

"I said, I used another man's property." The mockery in his eyes was as ugly as his voice.

"I haven't *any idea* what you're talking about. I'm no man's *'property.'* "

"No?" Alex's eyes were narrowed, skeptical.

"*No.* In fact, I—"

"Alex, Daddy has a question." Cecile's sudden, bright

presence was like sun shining on two thunderheads. "Is anything wrong?"

Alex spun around and wordlessly started off. Cecile started after him, but Erin caught her arm. There was only one explanation.

"Cecile, what have you told Alex about your father and me? I know you've told him something."

Cecile looked at her strangely. "Erin, I rarely talk to Alex about you at all. Why *would* I?"

"You've said something about Van and me. You must have."

"Well, naturally I told him Whitewater was your wedding present." Cecile shrugged. "He's known that for ages."

"Cecile." The valley seemed to tilt and Erin was sure she was going to topple over. What kind of people were these van Rijns? Expecting the world to fall in with whatever they had planned.

"Oh, come on, Erin. It isn't as if you didn't know. You've gone right along with it. Why else would Daddy let you design his house any way you chose? He's not all that generous."

Erin felt as if a bucket of cold water had been thrown over her, but she *hadn't* known. Of course she had wondered about the house; no one behaved as Van had without good cause. He had said he loved her, but . . . Good God. She felt as dumb as a hoe handle, and gullible.

"Oh, Cecile," was all she could say; she was overwhelmed.

"Oh, Erin." Cecile imitated her almost-wail and smiled a sweet smile. "You know you won't turn Daddy down. No one does. He's sweet, he's handsome, he's crazy about you"—the smile grew worldly wise—"and he's rich. Terribly rich."

"But I don't love him," Erin declared.

"That's *stupid*." Cecile glared at her, as though she couldn't believe her ears. "Hurting my father and throwing away all he can give you because you don't love him is silly. Maybe you'll end up loving him if it matters that much."

"And maybe I *won't*." Erin was feeling downright obstinate and she dug in her heels. "I don't think I'm being stupid at all. I'm being honest. And marrying Van without love would hurt him more in the long run."

"Oh, God," Cecile snapped, exasperated. "All right. You're not stupid, but you'd be crazy to throw all this away. And I know you're not crazy." Cecile gave her a long, penetrating look before storming off.

Erin decided angrily that it was high time she had a talk with Van. A long, sobering talk. Now wasn't the time, of course; the ride back to Shadyside would be too noisy, and he had already commented on his busy schedule the next several days. She'd just have to make an appointment with him.

She did so as soon as she returned to her office, and though the meeting was three days off, Erin now felt a vast sense of relief.

The office was busy, but once Erin was on the way home, her thoughts of Alex and the van Rijns surfaced, and were like leaves tossing every which way in the wind.

The most important thing was the misunderstanding, the terrible misunderstanding, between herself and Alex. Cecile had probably let that bomb about Whitewater being her wedding gift fall the day after she and Alex had made love. The day the two of them had driven all over creation in that rally.

When she reached home, Erin hurried to the telephone, eager to talk to Alex right away. She got his answering service and had to leave a message for him to call her instead.

She had just sat down to have a crisp tossed salad and hot rolls when she heard the clatter outside. Erin might have thought the roof was falling in had she not heard so many choppers lately. She nearly dashed outside before she remembered she was wearing only a bra and panties in her effort to keep cool. It had been one of the hottest days in August.

She raced upstairs and slipped on a pair of shorts and a cotton T-shirt before racing back down. When she reached the porch, Alex was crouched beneath the still-rotating blades and was headed for the house.

She gave him a small wave and a shy smile as he took in her bare legs and feet. He followed her into the kitchen, and in the deep quiet that followed the silencing of the chopper's engine, they stood looking at each other.

He still wore his work clothes, faded jeans and a navy T-shirt, but she noticed he had exchanged his muddy boots for comfortable leather sandals. He had come, it seemed, directly from Whitewater.

"I tried to call you. I left a message . . ."

She looked at his dark eyes, but only for an instant because the fire was there again and the current was sizzling between them. She fastened her gaze on his thin cotton shirt, but the muscular planes of his chest were too disturbing. It wasn't safe even to look at his arms. They were so brown and lean that she wanted to run her hands over them and play with the crisp sun-lightened hair on his forearms.

Oh, Lord, maybe she should just let well enough alone and not try to explain. Then things wouldn't get fired up again and she couldn't be hurt. Cecile could have him. How strange that she still liked Cecile in spite of everything.

"Repeat what you told me this morning," Alex said without preamble.

"I was just ready to eat. Are you hungry?" She indicated the salad and the basket of rolls. "Maybe we can have a civilized discussion for a change."

"Are you sure you have enough?" He scowled at the table.

"There's plenty. Sit down."

He nodded and did as she said. Erin felt his eyes examining her.

She popped the rolls into the toaster oven and calmly put down a second place mat and table setting. When the rolls were hot she put them in front of him.

"Help yourself." She started to sit down. "How about some wine? Burgundy? Chablis?"

"Burgundy's fine."

She went to the big pantry for the bottle and two glasses. When she poured the wine for him, her hands trembled. This meeting had come about so suddenly she hadn't had time to think, but now she realized they would be together and she would have to look into his eyes.

Alex helped himself to the salad and then buttered a crisp roll. He bit into it, chewed, and closed his eyes.

"Mmm."

When she saw he had mellowed considerably with just that one bite, Erin took a swallow of Burgundy, followed that with a deep breath, and plunged in.

"Cecile told me just this morning about Van's big plans for me," she began. "Wedding bells and Whitewater. Lord only knows what else she *didn't* tell me." She took a small sip of wine and nervously fingered the stem of the wineglass. "The prospective bride was never informed."

Alex's mouth twisted cynically, matching the disbelief in his eyes. "Is it standard," he asked, "to be given carte blanche with a house and design it however you want?"

"I suppose it is when the client is a man like Nicholas van Rijn and he says he loves you and . . ." Her voice trailed off. "Don't you dare smirk at me, Alex Butler. You don't know a thing about it."

"Tell me," he said gruffly, reaching for another roll.

"All right, I *will*." Her temper was mounting. "I had a bad case of puppy love for Van when I was sixteen, and I hadn't seen him since. Then he popped up in March and insisted I design his house. Later, to my surprise, he admitted that he loved me."

"So, you can have him after all. A fairy-tale ending." Alex tossed down the remainder of his wine.

"Hardly. I don't love him."

"But you allow him to kiss you," Alex pointed out as he picked up the bottle of Burgundy and scowled at it before refilling his glass. The wine had been a gift from Van and Erin was sure Alex knew it.

"I really can't imagine why you care if he kisses me. It's a delicate situation, his being an old family friend as well as a client."

"And influential."

"And influential," she admitted uncomfortably. There was no escaping the fact. "Naturally I don't want to offend him."

"Naturally. So you just lead him on and let him paw you. That's rational." He nodded agreeably and refilled his plate. "The salad's good, incidentally, and the rolls."

"I'm *not* leading him on," Erin declared, "and he's never pawed me. Even if he had, it's none of your business."

As they sat there eating and talking, Alex's overwhelming presence seemed to charge her cozy yellow kitchen with a dangerous electrical excitement, as though a live wire were loose and shooting off sparks.

"Ah, Kelly, I disagree."

He was jealous, she thought incredulously. Although the very thought warmed her, Erin hated to think how the situation must look to him. Van didn't paw—it wasn't his style. And she had never led a man on in her life. Not knowingly.

She finally put a bit of salad on her plate, but she couldn't eat. Damn. She wanted their relationship straightened out once and for all.

"You still haven't said *why* it should matter if Van kisses me. Or why you've been so *nasty* or . . ."

His eyes were suddenly on her, wide and unblinking. Deep, liquid, brown pools, hot, sensuous depths in which she could drown if she weren't careful.

"Why shouldn't I be 'nasty'? I make love to you and then find out you belong to Van."

His words were spoken quietly enough, but she sensed his underlying rage.

"There you go again." She threw her fork onto her plate. "I don't belong to Van or to anyone else."

He poured some Burgundy into her glass and refilled his own. "That's what I want to hear about. It's amazing that I should hear two such completely different stories."

She stared at him. "I can't believe this. Why should you take Cecile's word over mine?"

She watched him smile, watched all the little tension lines around his eyes and mouth smooth and relax. "Maybe I'll reserve judgment," he said.

"Well, that's certainly generous of you."

Were any man's eyes ever so hot and so tawny brown? she wondered unhappily. She remembered how warm his skin had felt against her own nakedness, and how the hard heavy length of him had pressed her into the old four-poster bed.

She quickly reached for a roll. "I'm glad you like the food," she said, out of the blue. "The rolls are called hearth rolls. They're a recipe of my mother's . . .'' She put all her attention on buttering the one in her hand.

"Look at me, Erin."

She did, defiantly. When he raised one black eyebrow in addition to the mocking smile on his lips, a color flushed her cheeks. No matter—she would stare him down. She took a bit of her roll and chewed, her eyes locked with his.

Nothing had been resolved at all, Erin thought ruefully. Tensions had been relieved a bit, yes, but Alex still didn't believe her, and she was angry and bewildered. She wanted him as much as ever, maybe even more, and she was angry and bewildered about that, too.

"I want to know you better." His voice had a husky edge.

"Well, you certainly have a strange way of showing it," she retorted, thinking unhappily that he already knew her intimately, and a lot of good that had done her.

"It was only this morning," he said gruffly, "that realized maybe you weren't a bed-hopper as I thought you were, that maybe you weren't cheating on Van."

"*Maybe?* You *beast*." She hurled her napkin at him and he caught it easily.

"What a spitfire." His laughter filled the room. "F'll concede you're a good cook and you have a bit of architectural ability. But I want to know more about you." Alex reached across the table and caught her hands, his eyes teasing. "Kelly, let's lie down and talk."

"I think not, Mr. Butler. We'll sit right here and talk. Or maybe you'd prefer the swing on the back porch?"

Every part of her was yearning for him, to taste and feel him again, to savor him, to inhale the sun-and-wind fragrance of his black hair and tanned skin. Erin fought her hunger silently, took another bite of roll, and gazed at him.

So. He wasn't completely sure of her? He would reserve judgment? Well, she wasn't sure of him when it came right down to it. Though his nastiness had been explained, Erin realized there was still a lot about this man she didn't know. His many women, for instance. Apparently it was all right for *him* to bed-hop—or had Cecile been wrong about that, too?

He was beside her then, pulling her into his arms. Erin reminded herself wildly that all he wanted was a fling. She had ignored that fact once and suffered; ignoring it a second time would be stupid.

"Alex, *no.*"

He lifted her off her feet so that her lips were on the same level as his, and that wonderful warm helplessness was invading her limbs. The delicious sensation that his touch inevitably commanded from her; softness and a warm, pliant yielding, a natural complement to his hardness and masculinity.

The fight was gone from her body, but Erin's brain still had a bit of spark left. "Alex, don't you hear?" she murmured against his mouth, "I said n—"

His hungry tongue stopped her words effectively as one arm slipped beneath her legs and swung her into his arms. She was being carried from the kitchen, his mouth still covering hers, and her heart leaped.

He brought her to the sofa, and she was childishly relieved it wasn't the bed. The sofa was safe; she could reason with him there. He wouldn't force her, she knew, but his tongue was another matter. Her mouth was being thoroughly and hungrily ravished by it.

He sat down and positioned her beside him, his arms about her, and her legs stretched along the length of the sofa. His long fingers caressed the skin under her clothes, teasing in and out of her bra, slipping beneath the lace and over the hard little buds tipping her breasts. Enticing and tantalizing her without hesitation.

Erin halfheartedly resisted him, trying to turn her head

from his harsh, plunging kisses, trying unsuccessfully to hold back his one searching hand while he held her other in a viselike grip. It was a game they were both enjoying, and she found his aggression exciting.

She began placing many small kisses on his neck and face, but in her uncertainty she still tried to stop his roving hand.

"What is you want, Erin, yes or no?" he growled. "We've played long enough."

"I . . . don't think we should." She wanted desperately to say yes, but was afraid.

"I suppose it's Van." His annoyance was evident.

"No, Alex, it's *not* Van. I just don't jump into bed this easily."

"Is that so?" He gently but firmly grasped both her wrists in his one hand and continued to explore her curves with his other. She shivered. Everywhere he touched her, her skin flamed.

"Alex, I *mean* it," she gasped as he pulled off her shirt. "We should stop."

"Uh-huh," he murmured, kissing her again.

She closed her eyes then, savoring the deliciously prolonged sealing of his lips on her own. It blotted out all her fears, and Erin could protest no more as he unfastened her shorts and pulled them down along her silken legs.

Pulling her wrists free of his grasp, she unhooked the little bra fastener and watched her breasts spill free into his eager hands.

His mouth tasted the hollow of her throat, the tip of her nose, which he then nuzzled with his own, the curves of her shoulders, and finally, the deep, sweet valley cupped between his hands.

"Oh, Alex." She lay her hands on top of his, encouraging them now.

Alex stood and pulled her to her feet, holding her in such

a way that the tips of her breasts rubbed sensuously against his chest. "Woman, I'm taking you up to bed." His eyes glittered over her ivory lace panties before he gave her a light whack on her small, rounded derriere. "What will it be? Over my shoulder—the fireman's carry—or in my arms? *Quick.*"

"You'll have to catch me first." She darted off toward the kitchen, laughing, but she was deeply aroused by his strength and the passion she saw in his eyes. She craved more.

"This had better be fast," Alex said, and he was after her like lightning. He easily caught her and pulled her back to the living room. He pinned her back to his stomach, spooning her against him, his arms circling her from behind with one hand claiming a breast as the other caressed the softness between her legs.

She laughed, a husky sound from deep in her throat. She was amused yet terribly excited by the way his hands were holding her, claiming her. They seemed to say she was his. Totally his . . .

Alex's warm breath nuzzled the back of her neck in a whisper. "You little siren, now are you satisfied? I've caught you." He turned her around, his hot eyes enjoying the sight of her breasts pressed against his chest.

"Completely satisfied." She, too, was whispering. Erin stood on tiptoe, tilting her head back to offer him her willing mouth. "You've caught me." She brushed her lips over his, then began to slip his T-shirt up, exposing his hard, tanned chest. "Now I seem to be completely at your mercy." This time her mouth teased over his hard nipples.

He stepped back to pull off his shirt, then flung it to the floor. Erin's arms went around his waist, her hands sliding down his back, stroking his bare skin and slipping beneath his jeans, down over his taut, cool buttocks to press him hard against her.

"God," he gasped. "Who's at whose mercy?"

She felt his growing excitement against her belly and saw his brows meet as though in exquisite pain. His hands smoothed over her skin as he lowered his head so his lips could brush her shoulder.

"You're as soft as velvet."

Alex's breath was short and harsh as she unzipped his jeans and helped him shake his long brown legs free of them. She trailed kisses over him then, over his chest and up his throat and along the square line of his jaw. She stopped abruptly before she reached his lips and gave him an impish grin.

"I've changed my mind. I think I'll get dressed."

He was laughing at her playful efforts to free herself, laughing and holding her small white naked body firmly imprisoned in his arms, drawing her closer and closer until they seemed nearly one even as they stood there.

Alex lowered her to the sofa, his hungry eyes and hands moving over her, shifting her to her back, gently parting her legs. She gasped. She had never made love in her living room before.

"Alex, are you sure you don't want to—"

Quick and sweet and smooth as a sigh, he took her, and was caught in that warm, tight prison between her legs. Eyes closed, her lips kissing his eager mouth, Erin immediately felt his rapid thrusting deep within her.

She had teased and tormented him so that there was a frenzied urgency to his movements. She in turn was so excited that her body's own response to him—a deep, luscious tension, a tension growing and mounting to a hot, hard peak and then exploding into fiery ecstasy—made Alex arch his body again and again as he moaned with pleasure.

When at last they lay quietly in each other's arms, damp and exhausted, Erin was completely content. Alex's lovemaking was every bit as wonderful as she had remembered.

The telephone rang and she stirred slightly, but Alex's arms tightened, holding her against him.

"Don't answer."

"Alex, I have to. Just let me see who it is and then I'll get rid of the caller. I can take the phone off the hook."

She caught the phone in mid-ring and carried it back to the living room. It was Van, and she was too befuddled to think straight.

"*Van.* Oh, hello . . ." She knew immediately she shouldn't have said his name.

Erin watched as Alex's now-familiar mask replaced the sensuous contentment on his face. It was as though an ice storm had swept through her house.

She covered the mouthpiece and whispered, "Alex, I'll only be a minute," and then, "Yes, Van. Of course."

She spoke only briefly, but when she hung up, she felt the chill all the way across the room. Alex had risen and was dressing.

She went to him and slipped her arms around his waist. "You're not leaving . . ." She leaned her head against his chest and heard the slow, solid beating of his heart.

His mask was still in place as he removed her arms from around him. "Yes, I think I'll head for home."

Damn him, she thought, for having the power to hurt her so much. She felt ridiculous standing there naked and unwanted.

"Well, it seems I needn't have hung up."

"So it seems. Why not call him back right now?"

"I think I *will*."

His eyes flickered over her dangerously. "Erin, I'm not a sharing man."

So there it was. With all his talk about reserving judgment, he hadn't. He didn't believe her at all.

"Thanks for dinner. I enjoyed it." His eyes moved over her again. "And I enjoyed you . . ." Subconsciously Erin had already assumed a classic pose, her arms and hands protecting her nakedness from masculine eyes.

Alex strode out the front door, whereupon she retrieved her shirt and shorts from the floor and put them on. She listened as the chopper engine started, the blades began beating the air, and then he was gone. Her heart went with him.

She slowly walked through the rooms in which the two of them had sat and talked and made love, but they seemed dark and empty even with the light of the setting sun streaming in. It was as though every lamp in the house had been lit, giving it warmth and excitement, and now . . . now they had all been turned off.

Chapter Nine

In addition to her empty feeling, Erin was stung over Alex's anger and unfairness. When she returned Van's call, she almost took it out on him. It was his fault, after all, that Alex had stormed out of her house, his fault that Alex didn't trust her.

She was so cool, so insistent on seeing Van as soon as possible, that he agreed to an appointment the very next day. It so happened he'd be in Shadyside on business.

"It sounds unpleasant enough, my dear, that I want to get it over with."

Traffic next afternoon was terrible, practically bumper to bumper all the way from Center Avenue to Walnut Street. When Erin finally entered her office, late for Van's appointment and upset because his time was valuable, she discovered Van and Deirdre having a delightful tête-à-tête over iced coffee and petits fours.

"Darling," Deirdre chirped. "You poor thing, out in that wretched heat. Here, have a tall glass of iced coffee. Are you hungry? She looks peaked, doesn't she, Nicholas?"

"I'm fine," Erin said as she sank down in front of the fan and gratefully accepted a frosted glass of cream-laced coffee and a petit four from her sister. "Have you two had a good talk?" She had noticed Deirdre's glowing face.

"I am delighted to make this lovely lady's acquaintance

once again,'' Van said gallantly. "We've been discussing old times, my sweet.''

About time, Erin thought as she crunched on an ice cube and led him into her office. She'd been trying to arrange a get-together between Deirdre and Van for weeks.

She set the whirring fan on low, sat down at Quintus Corcoran's old desk, and took another swallow from her glass.

"Van . . .''

"My sweet?''

Instantly she was annoyed. "I *wish* you'd call me Erin.'' It wasn't a good beginning.

Van took out a cigarette, put it in an ebony-and-gold holder, and lit it. "Very well. Erin.'' He looked down at his watch.

"I want you to be honest, Van. What do you expect of me?''

He raised both eyebrows. "As to what, my dear? House design? I'm perfectly satisfied, and I believe I can arrange a meeting with Punch Scanlon so that—''

"*Van.*'' She put her glass down on a coaster. "Cecile seems to think you want to marry me. She also seems to think Whitewater is to be my wedding gift. Now, I'll feel awfully silly mentioning this if none of it's true. Just about as silly as I'll feel if it *is* true.''

"And that's what this is all about?'' He chuckled. "This very important meeting?''

"*Is* it true?''

"My dear, you look like a *gamine* today. You're completely charming when you're so flushed and tousled. And that's a very attractive dress—white becomes you.'' Seeing her growing irritation, he added, "Yes, I suppose I might have mentioned something of the sort to Cecile.''

"Oh, Van, *why*? I don't intend to marry again for a long time.''

"My dear, that's no problem. I'll wait."

"Van, there *is* a problem. I like you, I'm extremely fond of you, but . . ."

"But you don't love me." He smiled matter-of-factly and he didn't seem hurt in the least. "Love is not a prerequisite for marriage to me, Erin. I should have made that clear much sooner . . ."

"It's as though he has a wall around him," Erin complained to Deirdre after Van had left. "A wall that prevents him from seeing the way things really are. I told him three times I wouldn't marry him, and do you know what he said?"

"No, darling, what?"

"He said, 'Women are changeable, my sweet. You'll no doubt change your mind.' He hadn't paid a bit of attention to a word I'd said."

"Erin, calm yourself, dear. It's much too hot to get worked up and you're getting all pink!"

"Deirdre, what's happening? He's taking me for granted, but *I'm* the one who feels guilty."

"Why?"

"Because I think I've . . . well, maybe I've led him on." The thought hadn't occurred to her until Alex had mentioned it. Erin began to pace nervously about.

"I've been so grateful for the commission and I love the house so much that my feelings for Whitewater may have overflowed. And I haven't wanted to be too stiff with him or hurt him, and he's misinterpreted that."

She sank to the floor in front of the fan and allowed it to blow air over her, whipping her hair about and soothing her hot skin. Erin wished she could slip out of the white cotton suit she wore and into something cool. She compromised by taking off her shoes.

"What do you do with a man who won't take no for an

answer?" she wailed. "Who just chuckles good-naturedly and thinks you'll 'come around'? I don't think a woman has ever refused him before. And I can't just *not* see him, not while the house is going up."

"Darling, you should be very careful about all of this. Don't do anything rash or foolish. Most women would love to have Nicholas, you know. He's so gallant and good-looking, and has such marvelous Old World manners."

Manners that included hand-kissing, Erin thought wryly. Deirdre adored that, and was still starry-eyed over Van's parting performance with her, although he'd left half an hour ago.

"And he can give you everything," Deirdre added, "anything and everything."

"But we have nothing in common," Erin lamented. "I like the country, he likes the city. He likes parties, I like peace and quiet. I like my old, ratty clothes, and he always looks like a fashion plate." She shook her head. "He's your type, not mine."

"Oh, dear. Well—Whitewater, then?"

"Not even Whitewater. Give up, love. Nicholas van Rijn isn't for me. Let me give him to *you*."

"Oh, darling, please do."

Actually, it was his attitude toward the house that made Erin the unhappiest about Van. His heart and sweat and tears hadn't gone into it, so naturally she couldn't complain about that, but he had never agonized or even exalted over it. She had seen him mildly excited once or twice for a few minutes, but that was all. No, he'd been at the peak of his enthusiasm when she said she would design it. Nothing since. He'd supplied the money, mere petty cash for Nicholas van Rijn.

It was early October when the van Rijns, father and daugh-

ter, were called to New York for two weeks. Van had
offered Erin the use of his chauffeured car should she happen to visit the site, but when she did decide to go, she
took Mighty Mouse.

She was pensive as she drove, thinking how she had seen
Alex frequently—once a week being frequent when both
of them were running from morning till night. Things
seemed to be a bit better between them, more on an even
keel. They weren't sniping at each other, but they were
cautious. She didn't want to be hurt and he—Erin
shrugged and shifted down on the rocky road to Laurel
Bluff—Lord only knew about Alex.

He wasn't in sight when Erin arrived. She greeted the
men pleasantly and moved downhill toward a spot where
she could look up at the house and savor it; savor the day
in general, with its clean, crisp wind and blue sky. And
face it, Erin Kelly, she thought a bit sadly, savor Van's
absence. It was just too bad she wasn't like those women
Deirdre talked about, women who'd give their eyeteeth to
marry Nicholas van Rijn. That would certainly simplify her
life, but it was years too late.

As she shuffled through the leaves, red and orange and
burgundy, dappled with sunlight and dew, Erin began to
enjoy the spectacular display of nature all around her.

She was standing under a golden red canopy of maples
that made everything and everyone beneath them glow,
and the valley floor was a vivid contrast with the deep
greens of laurels, hemlocks, and rhododendrons. Through
the middle, Otter Run was chuckling quietly down to the
lake. The lake itself, blue as forget-me-nots, was rimmed
on the far side by masses of yellow trees, and the fall fragrance of woodsmoke and dried leaves teased her nostrils.
What a marvelous fall day.

She turned then and looked up at the house. Things had
come a long way for her baby. Whitewater's brown shin-

gled roofs now plunged and disappeared into the surrounding red-gold wonderland; graceful, floating planes that softened the lines of the house and induced a warm sense of shelter.

Wooden scaffolding was still in place beneath the cantilevers, however, protecting the bedroom wing, which soared out over Otter Run and the first- and second-floor terraces.

Whitewater was nearly finished, and Erin could easily visualize it without those supporting timbers. Soon it would be fully grown and strong, this child of hers, able to stand on its own. She felt a thrill of pleasure. No matter what she designed in future years, Van's forest home would always be the love of her career.

The music from Otter Run covered the rustle of approaching footsteps, and Alex was beside her before she saw him.

"She looks mighty good." he smiled down at her.

Erin nodded, pleased. "She does. I wasn't sure you were here. I saw the helicopter, but I thought you might have driven to town."

"I've been down at the lake," he said. "Goofing off." He pointed to a fishing rod standing against a nearby tree. "I don't work every single minute I'm here, you know."

His eyes took in her small form clad in colorful fall attire, plaid slacks, a deep green sweater, and a beige corduroy jacket thrown over her shoulders. She sensed he was in a happy mood, actually glad to see her. Erin watched as he retrieved his fishing rod, then they rustled noisily uphill through the leaves.

Her heart was singing because he had looked at her with such evident pleasure in his eyes. Well, she might as well enjoy it while it lasted, she thought. Enjoy this tall, good looking man with his black hair and brown eyes vivid against his red plaid shirt and khakis.

"I have one last thing to say about Van," she blurted out, surprising herself. "He's only a good friend, no matter what you've heard or . . . continue to hear."

Alex nodded. "Sure." His eyes were suddenly distant and narrowed, making her wish she hadn't said anything. "You don't have to explain."

"But I *want* to explain. Van's used to having his own way." Like Cecile, she wanted to add. "Used to having people fall in with his plans. He doesn't take no for an answer, but he's so gentle and bland that it's hard to fight back." Those beautiful flowers that had come yesterday, for instance.

Alex's eyes were on the house. Perhaps his thoughts were, too, Erin mused sadly. He seemed far away. It was as though he had his own wall built around himself; she hadn't made him understand.

"Have you been in the house yet today?" he asked.

"Not yet."

He took her arm and led her over the uneven humps of earth, into the house, and up the stairs to the second-floor terrace.

"Now, Kelly, don't get upset about this—"

"Alex, what *is* it?"

"Nothing much, but I figured you'd be unhappy." He pointed to a network of fine cracks in both the floor of the terrace and the surrounding parapet, watching as she gaped at them. "It's all right, you know. It's minor and there's no cause for concern."

"Negative moment," she murmured finally, and put both hands to her face. It was inevitable to have some droop in a beam that had a great amount of stress above its point of support, but she had calculated so carefully. Her perfect child had its first blemish.

"It won't weaken the concrete, Erin."

"I know."

"And having cracks is the nature of the beast—of concrete, that is."

"Yes."

"The only way we could have avoided it would have been to put expansion joints in the cantilevers, and we didn't want that."

"They would have been ugly," she whispered as his hands went to her shoulders and squeezed them. "Uglier than the cracks."

"*Hell.* No problem. We'll hide them. We'll smooth them over with—" He stopped, tilted her chin, and looked down into her face as she struggled not to weep. Alex kissed the tip of her freckled nose and said quietly, "Go ahead, Erin, cry. I know how you feel."

The cracks were disappointing but minor, as he'd said. It was Alex's gentle, unexpected concern that was so devastating. If he could be so sweet and sensitive some of the time, why couldn't he be that way all of the time? Why did he have to be so contrary and unpredictable that she never knew from one moment to the next when his mask would go on again?

The tears came freely then, and his arms wrapped around her as though they'd never let her go. Erin's tears made a large wet spot on the front of his plaid shirt. "You—you'll have to change your shirt," she sputtered.

It was so wonderful having his strength and comforting presence to draw on that she could barely breathe. She felt as if she were being enfolded, protected. Had Carl ever done this?

She heard his deep voice rumbling in her ear. "Erin, Erin, Erin." He kissed the top of her bright head. "It's a great house."

She enjoyed his arms around her a bit longer and then pulled back. "Thank you." She gave him a watery smile. "I don't normally cry over my mistakes." That was true, but he needn't know that he was the real reason for her anguish.

They went inside and she marveled that the glow from the sun-drenched maples seemed to follow them, bathing them in a rosy light, just as planned when she was designing Whitewater.

As Erin and Alex moved about the house they agreed that cold weather would be upon them before they knew it, and they discussed the things to be done during the winter months: window sashing, the woodwork and flooring, the cabinetwork.

When he pointed out the things that had been added since her last visit, Erin couldn't believe the light in his eyes. He *liked* her house . . .

He showed her the ruggedly handsome floor of the entry hall. "These flagstones will look just like bedrock when they're sealed and polished. Now come and look at this."

He took her hand and rapidly dragged her along behind him toward the den. "Lady, feast your eyes on that masterpiece. Danadio just finished it yesterday."

"Why, it's magnificent." She gazed, enthralled, at the massive, beautifully detailed fireplace of reddish stone. It was deep and wide enough to hold a simmering kettle of soup or a yule log; a perfect complement to the boulder top that thrust several inches above the wide, pegged floorboards to form a sprawling, seven-foot-long hearth. It was an awesome reminder of the site's glacial heritage.

"Shall we seal our boulder, Kelly?" Alex had knelt and was stroking it with both hands. "Nope, better not," he answered his own question. "Leave it natural." She turned away to hide her grin. It was perfectly clear that the boulder over which they had battled was no longer "her" boulder, it was "their" boulder.

Whitewater was their joint creation, the exhilarating

result of their hard work and worry and strain, though these hadn't been shared between them until recently.

What a change from those first five months. Erin had been afraid to open her mouth then. She had, of course, but always with a chip on her shoulder, and with good reason: he'd delighted in shooting her down. That young red maple, for instance . . .

She looked out to where it thrust up through the living-room terrace, graceful and colorful as it anchored the house more firmly to the earth. They'd had a battle royal over that until Van had put his foot down and Alex had had to give in and build around it, grumbling at the extra cost, time, and trouble.

But recently he'd grown amenable, sometimes even admitting sheepishly that many of his initial worries had been unfounded. And she'd discovered, when Van had told her, that there were many nights that Alex didn't return home, but stayed in his small trailer on the site.

Now it was all clear. He liked the house. The only thing that would have made her happier was if he'd come to like her as well. And believe her.

"When are you doing the stress tests?" she asked as they stood looking out at the stream and the woods. Stress tests on the cantilevers were the next major step.

"Within the next two weeks. I was going to call today and arrange it. Probably October twelfth or so." He saw her expression. "Hey, you're not worried, are you?"

"I'm terrified."

His arm dropped over her shoulder as they walked outside. Erin suspected he had no idea how his touch affected her, even such a friendly gesture as this.

"Well, don't be. If your consultant and my engineers are satisfied, don't lose any sleep over it."

But the test would tell all, and she would lose sleep, she knew.

"I want to be here, Alex. I'll help."

"You?" He grinned down at her.

"Why not?"

"How good are you at hauling bags of sand and cement?"

"Well . . ."

"Ninety-four pounds each."

Erin grinned. "*Try* me."

"You can't weigh much more than that yourself."

"*Ha.* Now tell me about the testing."

"We'll load the bags, as many as we have, and anything else that's heavy, onto the farthest extremities of the cantilevers. We pile on more weight than they'll ever have to bear under normal circumstances."

"And then remove the scaffolding?"

"And then remove the scaffolding." His dancing eyes studied her. "And then take sightings on the deflections."

She sighed. "I wish it were all over."

"Or never had to happen." He smiled gently.

She nodded, dreamy-eyed for a moment. "Well, I guess I'd better be getting back."

"Lots of work?" he asked, walking her to her car.

"Almost more than I can handle. Van has brought me so many jobs." She wished she hadn't mentioned Van. It made her seem so much closer to the man than she really was.

"Say, what's happened?" He was critically eyeing the Saab. "Is this a new car?" His eyes flickered over the car and then over her flushing cheeks, finally fastening on her wide eyes.

"I've just put some money into it. New tires and everything that was necessary under the hood. I got rid of all that rust, too, you'll notice." Mighty Mouse was gleaming with a new coat of paint. "You got me to think-ing. It's a good little car and I really had neglected it."

The truth was, every time she had some new thing done, she'd contemplated Alex's pleasure. Mighty Mouse no longer reminded her of Carl but of Whitewater's builder.

"I'm impressed." There was a look of thoughtful approval on his face.

She shrugged. "Well, all this cost far less than a new car would have."

Alex opened the door for her and she slipped behind the wheel.

"Kelly—"

"Yes, Butler?" She threw him an impish smile.

"You remind me a lot of a girl I once knew." His voice was quiet. "In fact, you remind me almost too much."

A teasing reply was on the tip of her tongue until Erin saw that odd glimmer in his eyes and the sudden grimness of his mouth. She caught herself just in time. "Well, I'll blast off now," she said gently, sobered by his change of mood. "You will let me know about the test date?"

He nodded, the odd look still in his eyes. Sadness, she had always thought, but a dangerous look nonetheless. It made her want to take him in her arms and put his head on her chest to comfort him. Instead she turned Mighty Mouse around and headed for the highway.

Pennsylvania in the fall and jazz on the radio almost dispelled the pall Alex's mood change had cast over her. It had been a good visit and Erin was glad she'd gone, but a nagging little thought kept coming back again and again. She reminded Alex of a girl, he had said. Reminded him too much. Anyone with two eyes could see he'd been in love with her.

Alex called, as he'd promised, to say the tests would be

made at the end of the month, near Halloween instead of mid-October. Erin immediately called Van's office so his secretary could schedule the event; she was sure he would want to be in on the excitement. When he called her on his return from New York, she reminded him.

"I'll be going up the day after tomorrow around ten, Van, for the tests. Remember? I think we can be back by two or three." Actually, she wished she could go alone.

"You go ahead," he said, miraculously granting her wish. "I have an appointment with my tailor that day."

"Your tailor?" Erin couldn't believe her ears. During the summer, when nothing much was happening, they'd flown up to Laurel twice a week, but now, now that the cantilevers were to be tested, he wouldn't break an appointment with his tailor.

"Van, this is a big day. Are you sure you don't want to come?" She crossed her fingers. If he said no, she at least would have tried.

"My dear, I say too much is being made of nothing. If the cantilevers droop, they droop. Put a pole or two under them to prop them up. I don't consider it a great problem."

Deirdre, putting a cup of hot chocolate on the oak desk in front of Erin, saw her eyes blaze. She mouthed a "What?" but Erin angrily shook her head. Deirdre would have to wait.

"Prop them up with poles?" Her voice was dangerously quiet, but Van didn't recognize the storm warning. Deirdre did and she sat down, staring at her sister while she listened.

"Poles, beams, any kind of reinforcement would completely spoil the floating effect of the cantilevers," Erin said coolly, "and the fact that there's no visible means of support. Anything like that would be ugly."

"Nonsense," said Van. "You're much too serious

about all this. I never meant, when I asked you to design a house for me, that you should spend your every waking moment on it and worry so about it. I expected us to see each other more often, get to know each other again."

"I see."

"And you must admit that every time I've asked you out recently, you've been doing some refinement or adaptation. Erin, the place is fine as is. Leave well enough alone."

Aside from the fact that she'd been avoiding Van, what he said was true. She had been fussing with the final details, wanting Whitewater to be as good as she could possibly make it.

"I'm sorry, Van, I don't work that way. I can't stop until it's perfect."

He sighed and tried another tack. "Did my flowers arrive?"

"Yes, and I'm sorry. I meant to thank you. They're beautiful. But I wish you hadn't." She had given up telling him not to send her flowers and wine and candy. As it was, she gave most of the things to Deirdre.

"I think you should accompany me to New York for the Thanksgiving weekend," he declared suddenly. "I want you to relax and allow me to pamper you, my dear. In my Manhattan town house. I also have tickets for two of the best shows on Broadway, and we can do whatever else your heart desires."

Erin was clutching the receiver so tightly she had a nasty cramp in her hand. "Van, I can't possibly."

"I have servants there," he added stiffly after a long pause. "If you're worried about being chaperoned, that is."

She shot a wild look at Deirdre and began to shake her head. "Van, you know that's not it. I've tried to tell you over and over: I'm *not* your fiancée, I'm not even your girlfriend. Please don't act as though I am." What in heaven's name could she do, short of insulting him outright, to turn him off and onto someone else? Deirdre, preferably.

"My dear, I'm tiring of this pursuit." His voice was querulous for the first time. "You're being very difficult. I realize that New York is rather ordinary. If you'd prefer Europe or Mexico for several weeks, say so. It can be arranged."

"I'm sorry," she said, growing more stubborn by the second, "but no."

"I, too, am sorry. All along I've thought that you would become reasonable—knowing, as you do, how I feel about you."

"I'm sorry about that, too. I really am. But you hired me to do the house, Van, and nothing else."

"I hired you, my lovely lady, because I wanted an excuse to be with you. To get to know you better. To court you. *Not*," he declared emphatically, "because of your ability."

"Why, why Nicholas van Rijn!" Each new admission was worse than the preceding one. "I can't believe you'd *do* such a thing."

"What thing?" Deirdre whispered, and Erin angrily shushed her.

"And I can not, absolutely can *not*, understand your obstinacy, my dear. Never have I met such a contrary female."

Erin sat up straighter in Quintus Corcoran's big swivel chair. So, that explained his sudden decision to build a house after holding the land for ten years. It also explained his lukewarm interest in Whitewater and his earlier insistence on visiting the site twice a week, come rain or shine. Erin expelled an angry breath. Why, he could have made do with one of Alex's third-rate architects and not noticed the difference.

"I see," Erin was so angry she was in danger of insulting him, valuable client though he was. She pushed the hold button and thrust the telephone at Deirdre.

Deirdre gasped. "What shall I tell him?"

"*Anything.*" Erin snapped. "If I said what I'm thinking, I'd only be sorry later on."

"Oh, Erin—"

"Make *any* excuse." Erin drummed her fingers angrily on the desktop as her sister, her blue eyes huge with confusion, spoke into the mouthpiece.

"Nicholas? This is Deirdre. Ah . . . Erin is, well . . . Erin is having a coughing fit. Oh, no. Nothing like that, my dear. Just a bit of phlegm in her throat. I'm so sorry, but you'll have to finish your conversation with her later. She's . . . quite incapacitated."

The conversation continued until Deirdre said, "Yes, darling. I'll tell her. Yes . . . yes . . . Good-bye."

When Deirdre hung up, she fixed stern eyes on Erin. "And good-bye, Nicholas van Rijn," she said. "He's been very patient, you know, and now he's terribly provoked with you. What in the world was that all about?"

"Oh, he makes me so mad," Erin fumed. "Planning things around me without asking if I'm interested, taking it for granted I'll go off with him for a weekend, and then . . . *then* admitting that he commissioned me just so we'd be together."

"But, darling, it's positively romantic that he cares so much."

"*Romantic.* Deirdre, am I crazy or are you?" Erin finally took a sip of her hot chocolate.

"Not crazy, dear, just independent. Cocky and independent. The way you were even as a small child. Oh . . . I almost forgot. Nicholas said to tell you that Cecile won't be at Whitewater for your droop test either. He's sending her off to Dallas on business . . . Erin, what's a droop test?''

Chapter Ten

And so Erin drove to Laurel alone. She briefly considered calling Alex for a ride in the chopper, but she hated to impose and couldn't quite make herself do it. Besides, she liked the freedom to keep her own pace and look at all the pale russet and wheat colors that told of winter's approach.

Snow fences had sprung up since her last drive there, and the corncribs were filled. Even the sky was wintry, with black clouds scudding east. Erin had always loved winter, and now she was filled with a wonderful sense of impending excitement. It made her briefly forget her reason for going to Laurel.

When she arrived, the loading of the cantilevers was nearly done. She sighed as she watched Alex effortlessly heave one bag after another to his shoulder and place it among the others collected on the first-floor terrace. Men. So strong and beautiful and . . . necessary.

"Kelly." Alex hailed her happily when he saw her.

"Hi. I'm sorry I'm too late to help."

"Too late? Who said so? You can start on those iron pipes. They're not too heavy."

She grinned as she marched off toward the stack of pipes. No mollycoddling of females from him. *Oof,* they *were* heavy. She squatted and rose, the end of one pipe clutched in both hands as she dragged it toward the first-floor terrace. All in all, she made twelve trips, and was almost ready to drop when the last pipe was placed.

Actually, Erin was glad to have something to do—anything to keep her mind off the impending tests.

"Are you going to make it?" Alex touched her arm gently.

She laughed. "Sure." She shrugged, then shuddered lightly.

"It's cold, just standing around." His eyes swept over her, approving of her pale blue sweater, navy jacket, and beige corduroy slacks. "Come on over to the fire."

She followed him to the large metal barrel where a fire was burning, a fire fed by scrap wood and cardboard. He unscrewed the lid of a half-gallon Thermos and poured her a cup of steaming black coffee.

"Bless you." She gave him a grateful smile and sank onto a log within warming distance of the heat. Her toes and fingers were freezing, and one little tremor after another shook her body.

Alex poured coffee for himself while he studied her. "Hell, Kelly. Why did you come today? Where's your . . . where's Van?"

She blinked, knowing he had been about to say "fiancé."

"I'm here because I couldn't stay away, and Van is having a fitting at his tailor's." She stared into the murky dregs of her cup, whereupon Alex filled it again.

"Seems to me you'd have been better off helping with the fitting."

She raised her eyes to his. "I'd rather know the worst right away, I guess."

He shook his head. "There won't be any worst, Erin, I promise you that." He sat down beside her, close enough that his hard leg brushed hers and she could feel his warmth.

If only he were right. No matter what she said, Erin really didn't want to know the worst. Not at all. She felt like such a child.

But she wasn't a child. She was an adult, an architect. She alone was responsible for the total design of Whitewater, for the possible folly of having built the structure over a gigantic boulder and cantilevering one wing over what might be a wild cascade of water when it stormed.

She'd gotten her own way in spite of Alex's objections, and now she was afraid. A simple error or wrong calculation on her part could mean a costly correction. She alone would bear the brunt of the consequences if she were wrong.

"Kelly." He was looking at her and shaking his head in wonder at her unhappiness, almost crooning her name, coaxing her to relax. "What's the worst, the absolute worst, that can happen?"

"The worst?" She threw one twig up into the fire barrel, then another. "The very worst," she said, laughing, "would be if everything fell down when the scaffolding is gone."

"So, we disregard that. Now, what else?"

"Well, if the stresses are too great and there's too much deflection, cracks will develop . . ." Her voice trailed off.

"Right. That's the worst, and it's a reasonable worry. Now, how would you attack that problem?"

"Direct vertical supports under the beams and the joists that are overstressed."

"Right. And there's no doubt in my mind you'd come up with something clever and unobtrusive. Something that wouldn't spoil the nice, floating effect you've achieved."

"I suppose you're right."

"*Hell*, Kelly, of *course* I'm right. So, what's the problem? You'll do what you have to do."

Looking into his warm, intelligent eyes made her feel as if she were floating. Erin gave him a wobbly, appreciative smile. How ironic that she should be hearing such words from the builder of that awful-looking mall, whereas Van, whose house it was, wasn't at all concerned about how it looked.

Her talk with Alex was a help, but still, when the dismantling of the scaffolding began, Erin left. She couldn't bear to watch.

She walked down the path to the lake and north along the grassy shore. Finding a smooth log, Erin sat down, trying to ignore the distant rumble: sledgehammers against wood, then the slam of wood against earth as the trembling beams fell to the ground. She looked at her watch. The engineers were due in fifteen minutes, but were such people ever on time?

She knew Whitewater was solid. Solid as the great boulder it had for a heart. Still, she could imagine the beams buckling, the steel-reinforced concrete crumbling and cracking once the supports were gone.

The distant sounds finally ceased and Erin froze, listening and hardly breathing. Nothing. No thunderous crash, only the quiet one might encounter waiting for a call in the night.

She took a deep breath, then another, as she felt her heart calming. Everything had been fine all along, but she did have a negative imagination . . .

Erin lost track of time walking along the lake, skipping stones into the water with her mittened hands, watching birds fly and the black clouds sail across the horizon. She finally turned and went back; she should know something soon.

She heard Alex then, heard him before she saw him. He was bounding down the hill and shouting her name.

"Erin, wait up."

Her heart swelled in a great blossoming beat at the sight of him. Pain and joy at the same time. God, she loved him . . .

"I don't suppose you care to hear?" He was so somber she was sure the worst had happened. She put both blue-mittened hands to her cheeks.

"Alex, please don't tease me," she whispered.

"They won't submit their final report until all the floors are laid." His dark eyes were suddenly dancing. "But the deflection for all three cantilevers fell well within the accepted limits. There's even a large safety factor. Great reserve strength."

"Oh, *Alex*." His words were such a thrill and a relief that Erin felt ten pounds lighter. But it was the excitement on his face that put the most joy into her heart. He was happy *for her*. Happy and proud.

When his long arms opened, she flew into them and they closed around her so tightly that she nearly cried out, but they felt so good. Unconsciously her lips were parting for his kiss, and then his firm mouth, warm and insistent, found them and tasted and sealed them for one long delicious moment.

As his lips sought her cheeks and her fluttering eyelids, Erin whispered, "We *did* it. Oh, Alex, we actually *did* it, didn't we?"

"Mm-hmm." He found her mouth again. It was obvious Alex had forgotten the house and the test, and planned to go on kissing her for some time to come.

She took a peek. His eyes were closed, the thick lashes resting on his tanned cheeks, and pleasure had softened the earlier tension lines in his face. She ran her fingers through his black hair, savoring the way it felt and how it curved about his temples and over his ears.

"How come you taste so good?" Alex pulled in a long, contented breath and once more drank deeply from the sweetness of her mouth, his hands pressing her small body to his own until she sensed his growing arousal. Finally he sighed and released her.

"We'll just have to wait, sweetheart. Save it for tonight." He gently cupped her breasts, seeming to claim them, then zipped up her jacket.

Erin looked up, startled. Her blue-green eyes darted over his face, searching . . . for what? Some sign that he finally believed her? That he wanted more than just a woman in bed? Wanted to make a commitment? But there was nothing other than hunger in his eyes, and, damn it, she could have stayed with Carl Kelly had that been all she wanted in a man.

She never did get to protest that he'd have to wait longer than tonight for her. He smoothed down her windblown hair, kissed the tip of her nose, and pulled the collar of her jacket up around her ears.

"Come and see the way she looks," Alex said, taking her small hand in his. He led her along the grassy shore and up the path that bordered Otter Run. Part way up, where the steepness ended and the valley leveled into one of the terraces, was the house.

Erin caught her breath.

Whitewater stood before them free and unencumbered, and for the first time she saw her child without its protective swaddling clothes, that network of awkward scaffolding. It was a perfect balance between the soaring terraces and the stone-and-redwood mass anchored to the ledges. Whitewater—a blending of nature and nest, wilderness and sanctuary. What a miraculous, lovely thing it was.

"I never dreamed . . . It's more beautiful than I could

have imagined." Nor could Erin have imagined the thrill of accomplishment that was surging through her at the sight of Whitewater, so strong and stable; finally able to stand on its own without help.

Alex nodded. "It's the best thing I've ever done." He was looking up at the house critically, through narrowed eyes, but Erin saw he was satisfied. That in itself was an accomplishment.

"We'll unload the weight now and put some of the timbers back," he said. "Some vertical supports, just to play it safe. The snow gets deep up here." He tousled the curls that he had smoothed minutes earlier, then caressed her cheek. It seemed as though he couldn't keep his hands off her. "Now, aren't you glad you came?"

"Oh, I guess so," she teased.

A workman strode up to Alex. "Miss van Rijn called while you were down at the lake, Alex." He looked at Erin a bit uncertainly. "She wants you to call right away. Something about her trip to Dallas being canceled, so she can see you tonight."

Alex's eyes went to Erin's face and she saw a flash of irritation in them. *He's sorry I heard that,* she thought sadly.

She looked at her watch. "Well, I'd better leave and let you get back to work."

"What about tonight?" Alex said as he caught her arm.

"What about Cecile?" she countered. "She said she could see you."

"She can see me out here anytime." There was a sharp edge to his voice.

"Well, I can't see you tonight, Alex."

"I'll be in touch, then," he said. "Tomorrow."

She shrugged. "I'm not in the office much. Don't be surprised if you can't reach me."

there was no excuse to visit the site as often. Or to see Alex.

But the house and its builder haunted her still, sometimes distracting her so much that she had to stop what she was doing, rub her temples, and start all over.

Alex hadn't invited her out again, though they spoke by telephone periodically. It was just as well, she thought, clinging to the rational, practical side of things. They had always squabbled and always would. Who needed it?

It was just before Thanksgiving when Deirdre reported seeing Van at a cocktail party.

"He looked so marvelous, darling. So *distingué*, I've always thought. I simply can't understand how you could not be attracted." She hung her beige cashmere coat on the clothes tree, poured herself a cup of coffee, and sat down at her desk. "*Brr*. It's really winter. Oh, before I forget, do you have plans for Thanksgiving?"

"Not yet." Erin hadn't given the holiday a thought and she sighed, keeping the sigh small, so Deirdre wouldn't notice.

When she and Carl had been married, the holidays had been unbearably exciting. In October she began planning her menus for both Thanksgiving and Christmas, wanting to make each year's celebration more wonderful and the food more delicious than the last. She'd made everything from scratch because her love for Carl had given her such an overflow of energy it could be harnessed for any amount of patient and painstaking effort.

She stood up abruptly and poured herself some coffee, pushing the festive smells and tastes and sights of holidays past into a cloudy corner of her mind.

"Erin." Deirdre's voice was so serious Erin gave her sister her full attention. "Going back to Nicholas—you haven't said a word about him for such a long time, dear.

Have you resolved you little spat? He was . . . quite attentive to me last night.''

Erin laughed. ''Heavens, Deirdre, *grab* him.''

''Darling, you're not being a martyr?'' When Erin hooted and lavished more coffee on her, Deirdre brightened. ''You don't mind?''

''Believe me, love, he's all yours. Actually, he was never mine to give.''

Deirdre said gently, ''You still love Alex, don't you?''

Erin picked up a pencil and directed her attention to the drafting board. ''I've given up on Alex.''

Van called Erin that very night, which was odd because he had been allowing her to do the calling, the reporting in. But now something was afoot; she could tell by his voice.

''Erin, my dear, how are you?''

''I'm fine, thank you, Van. How are you?'' It was a silly conversation, considering she'd spoken to him just that morning about the kitchen cabinets.

''I'm fit,'' was his brisk rejoinder, ''and I leave for New York Wednesday morning.''

''I hope you have a nice holiday.''

She had been about to make a pumpkin pie—she would have that, if nothing else festive, on Thanksgiving day—and as she waited uneasily for Van's next words she began to whip together the eggs, sugar, and spices.

After a long pause she finally said, ''Van? Are you still there?''

''Erin,'' he said then. ''Come with me. I promise you won't regret it.''

It was her turn to hesitate. He was sweet and dear and so many other good things that outweighed all his irritating little faults that it distressed her to say no again.

She sighed. ''Van, I—''

"My dear, I had to ask one more time. I won't press you." It was as though his mood changed then. "I saw Deirdre at a party last night."

"Yes, she mentioned seeing you. She enjoys your company so much."

They chatted for several minutes about Deirdre, and when Erin hung up, it was with a sweet sense of relief. She was certain that Van had just slipped out of her life, and unless she was completely mistaken, Deirdre would welcome him in hers. It was as though a puzzle piece had just dropped neatly into place. Now, she thought, if only the various facets of her own life would fit together as neatly.

When Deirdre called minutes later, Erin could barely hold her tongue in check. Deirdre would be so thrilled. But then would come the slow torture, waiting for Van to call. No, she decided firmly as she stirred the pumpkin in with the other ingredients while listening to Deirdre's chatter, she would keep her mouth shut. Let it all be a wonderful surprise if it happened, and if it didn't, well, at least Deirdre wouldn't have been disappointed.

". . . I've held off asking you until I checked with the Bishops, darling, and it's all right with them. You're invited there for Thanksgiving. They have a marvelous, ancient old farm near Chagrin Falls, all brass hinges and coach lamps. Horsy, of course, and very quaint. Do come. They're having scads in and one more won't make a bit of difference."

Erin stirred the pie filling and the wooden spoon made a comfortable plopping sound against the side of the bowl. She liked the Bishops, but the thought of spending the holiday with them made her enjoy more the thought of being home and alone.

It would be pleasant, with a fire crackling on the hearth and a chicken in the oven and the pie. Maybe a pecan pie, too. Erin sighed. She might have known she'd follow the traditional ritual. She had more good memories of past Thanksgivings to draw on than bad ones.

"You're sweet, Deirdre, and it's very nice of the Bishops. Thank them for me, but I really want to stay home."

"Home?"

"Home." Erin chuckled, knowing exactly the expression on Deirdre's face, and what she would be thinking: that her funny little baby sister hadn't outgrown all of her strange little quirks after all. "Home alone," she added.

Deirdre made protesting noises while Erin stirred three cups of milk, laced with cream, into the pumpkin mixture; it would be a pumpkin custard pie, her favorite.

It wasn't good to be alone on the holidays, Deirdre admonished her. It was just too depressing and, besides, Erin surely wouldn't want to make a feast just for one person.

"It's what I want, really."

"Well, if you're sure you won't be lonely, you must do whatever you think best. But I do hope you won't regret it, dear. And now I'll say Happy Thanksgiving, since I won't see you tomorrow. You remember I'm going to Cleveland first and then on to the Bishops'?"

"I remember," Erin said. "Have a wonderful time. Say hello to John and Kerry, and thank them."

"Yes, dear. Bye-bye."

"Good-bye. Happy Thanksgiving."

When Thanksgiving Day came, Erin didn't do a bit of what she'd planned. She had the one pie made, the stuffing ready to go into her chicken, and the old grinder was fastened to the counter, all ready to grind up cranberries and an orange, when she glanced out her kitchen window.

The sky had turned a dull pewter, and the tops of the maples and oaks scattered in the back fields were being whipped by a wild wind. It was the kind of day she had loved as a child, and she was filled with such a sudden yearning for things gone forever—the way they used to be—that she felt as gray and bleak as the sky.

Maybe Deirdre had been right. Maybe she should have gone along to the Bishops'. But did she really want to stand around with an artificial smile on her face and a cocktail in her hand? *No*.

Erin straightened her shoulders. All right, she told herself. Get the coffee made, warm the nut bread you made especially for this morning, and get a fire going. No moaning or moping. You refused Deirdre's invitation and now you're darned well going to cope.

When she wondered what Alex would be doing, the grayness within her seemed to expand. She opened the bag of coffee and was comforted by its fragrance, but only momentarily.

Images of Alex and Whitewater moved through her mind. Glimpses, shadows, snatches of things: fall colors; Alex in a red plaid shirt walking uphill beside her, toward where Whitewater stood cradled in the valley, so brave without its scaffolding. She hadn't been there since that day. Since Halloween . . .

She knew then that there wasn't another thing in this world she wanted as much as to see Whitewater.

Looking at the clock on the mantel, Erin saw that it was early. She would eat her breakfast, leave right away, and be home by two or three. Plenty of time to get dinner in the oven and have her Thanksgiving just as she'd planned. Why not? On a day when everyone else was with loved ones, it was appropriate she should visit Whitewater—her child.

Before she left, having a sudden inspiration, she tucked the pie and coffee makings into a small picnic basket. She would have her dessert at Whitewater.

Chapter Eleven

It was strange to see most of the equipment gone when she arrived at Laurel Lake. Strange, too, to be able to drive fairly close to the house on the small road that now branched off from the bluff road.

The weather had followed her. The sky was still pewter, and the russet leaves that lay on the ground like a carpet were being caught up here and there, twirling and dipping angrily over the valley.

Erin got out of the car and gazed hungrily at the house. Whitewater was all the sensuous colors of the earth. The rich brown of the roof, the honey beige of stone, the primitive red of the wood, the black slashes of the shadows that outlined its sweeping horizontal planes. How beautiful it was against a background of sandstones ledges and gray, naked branches that encircled it like etchings.

The supports were in place, just as Alex had promised, vertical timbers to prop up the farthest ends of the cantilevers during this first winter.

Erin, noticing a light inside, decided the workmen must have left it burning to discourage vandalism, not that there was much danger in this remote area. The light beckoned her warmly just as the first icy drops of rain began to fall.

She returned to the car to get her picnic basket, then ran quickly toward the house. There was a key, she knew.

Van and Alex had told her where it would be hidden in case she ever needed it, far back under the first-floor terrace, on a little ledge.

It was there, but so was something else. A gleaming gray Saab sheltered beneath the terrace from the weather. Alex's car.

Shaken, not knowing what kind of welcome to expect, yet filled with excitement, Erin ran for the back door. It was suddenly flung open and Alex's tall form took up most of the space. He quickly drew her in out of the wind and slanting rain, into the bright warmth of the kitchen.

"Alex, what in the world are you doing here?" She wiped raindrops from her face and threw back the hood of the blue jacket she was wearing.

"What about you, you poor waif? Have you no better place to be on Thanksgiving?" He took her coat and hung it in the closet.

"It so happens there's no other place I'd rather be." She grinned up at him, patted her hair into a semblance of neatness, then smoothed her rumpled clothing. She supposed she looked all right; her jade sweater, old though it was, was a pretty one and a nice complement to her brown tweed slacks.

She put her picnic basket on the kitchen counter. "You still haven't said why you're here."

"I had things to check over."

"Problems?"

The sudden, boyish grin he flashed at her made her knees feel wobbly. "I might as well admit it. There's no other place *I'd* rather be, either."

Her eyes widened. It didn't make a bit of sense. She'd always thought, without knowing why, that Alex's leisure time would be spent with a beautiful woman, skiing or sailing during the day and in each other's arms at night.

"There's no accounting for tastes," he added, his smiling eyes taking in all of her.

"Excellent taste, I say."

"How about some coffee?" He moved across the gleaming beige floor to his big Thermos which rested on the sink counter.

"I'd love some. And if you run out, I brought a coffee-pot and some coffee." The pie, she decided, would be a surprise for later.

He grinned and shook his head, as if enjoying a secret thought. "Come into the family room, Kelly. I have a fire going."

"I suppose you mean the den?"

"I stand corrected," he said. "The den."

She tagged after him, feeling very small as she gazed up at the breadth of his shoulders in the navy crew-neck sweater he wore. She wished those vague yearnings stirring deep inside her would disappear. It was plain as day that Alex liked her, but it was also clear that he was resigned to their platonic relationship. She certainly didn't intend to rock the boat.

The den, on this dark, rainy day, was a cozy lair with a bright, hot fire warming the boulder hearth.

"It's beautiful," she murmured, admiring her dream come to life. She could imagine how it would look with a braided rug and some furniture.

"Sit down and warm yourself." Alex dropped to a cross-legged position facing the fire, and so did she. Erin wished, ridiculously, that the hearth weren't so large. They could be closer together then, their knees touching . . . She sipped her coffee, staring at the tiny blue and green flames of the fire, pure and bright as cobalt and emerald as they licked the logs.

It was amazing, she thought. Here they were, sitting

atop the very boulder she had known must be part of the house.

"Amazing, isn't it?" Alex seemed to have read her thoughts. "I grumbled like hell about this boulder." He patted the warm surface beneath them.

"You certainly did." She laughed, feeling wonderfully vindicated by his admission. "But you were right to be cautious. And I'm thankful we extended the footings and thickened the walls. I sleep better—"

She quickly lowered her lashes. The word "sleep" was a loaded one, with him sitting there beside her. That night she had spent in his arms seemed almost a dream now. She took another piece of scrap wood from the pile at her left and laid it carefully on the fire. Alex, too, seemed to have a sudden need for activity.

"Are you hungry?" he asked, and when Erin nodded, he disappeared, only to return with a wedge of Brie, a box of crackers, and a big chocolate bar.

"I guess I knew I'd have company for Thanksgiving dinner," he said with a smile. Erin watched as he dug a Swiss army knife from his pocket and sliced a thin wedge of cheese for her. "Here. Dig in." He offered her the crackers.

She helped herself, wondering when cheese and crackers had tasted so good.

"Do you do this often?" Erin asked. "Come up here, I mean."

He nodded. "I like being here. I told you before but you've probably forgotten. This is one hell of a house, Kelly."

Forgotten? How *could* she have forgotten his unexpected but welcome praise? "Coming from you," she answered quietly, "it's wonderful to hear." Which didn't begin to describe how his words made her feel.

She smiled and gazed at him openly, enjoying without

embarrassment the sight of his handsome features. Finally, it seemed, they could be friends. Good friends. All things considered, maybe that was the best solution.

"Kelly, I've been meaning to tell you something." His eyes moved to hers. "This house is the first thing I've built that's given me a thrill. A real high. And you've taken a hell of a lot of criticism from me."

She decided he was under a strange spell. "I haven't exactly been the easiest person to get along with either."

Alex shook his head sharply. "You've been okay. I was tough on you. Extra tough. And you were right about my mall. It's the damnedest-looking thing I've ever built—"

"Alex, that was *terrible* of me."

She was laughing, she couldn't help it. She patted his hand, but he scowled and shook his head.

"Alex, *don't*. People will swarm to it and think it's wonderful." She herself was feeling wonderful; a warm, living, growing joy was spreading within her.

"I've always used the best materials," he said, "good men, and I move fast. I crack the whip." He gave the fire an angry poke. "But somehow I've let people with more money than sense have their way. I've given them what they wanted, and you've seen the result. Second-class stuff. But I hadn't cared until now."

Erin had thought she couldn't be more surprised until he added, "I was thinking of using a consultant the next time. An eminent authority."

"That's a *great* idea."

"Yup, the most eminent of the eminent," he said dryly, and now she saw the twinkle in his eyes. "Will you consult for Butler Builders, Ms. Kelly?"

Pleasure brightened her eyes and brought a pink glow to her cheeks. "I'd be honored."

He looked back at the fire and she saw he was satisfied. Erin had thought for a moment, when their eyes met, that he might hug her, but the moment was gone. She was glowing nonetheless, glowing inside and out. She wasn't sure how, but they seemed to have made a new beginning.

The conversation drifted back to Whitewater, a topic they both enjoyed.

"You say you like the house," Erin offered. "Well, I like the way you've done it. You're economical and efficient, and you're fast. Alex, you can build for me anytime."

Alex's smile nearly melted her bones. "The weather cooperated for a change, but I just might take you on as my PR person. And as I said a while back"—he tossed a stray twig on top of the flames—"Cecile was a big part of it. I don't know how she did it, but every delivery was on time. Maybe being a van Rijn was all it took."

When his eyes traveled over her, Erin realized he had thrown in Cecile's name to test her reaction. To test the water before taking the plunge.

"Cecile really found her métier on this job—being Van's representative. I suppose you know she's gone on to bigger things?"

"No, I didn't."

"I thought maybe Van had told you." He let fly another twig at the flames.

"I haven't seen Van for weeks," she said. "I report by phone."

Their eyes met briefly, a pure burst of electricity between them, and then she saw the slightest smoothing of his forehead.

"Tell me. What about Cecile?" Erin's curiosity was piqued.

"That little girl likes the feel of power. She gets it being 'Daddy's' representative."

Erin's eyes widened. Firelight was in them, turning

them gold-green and burnishing her hair until it gleamed
like mahogany.

"Well, what is she doing?"

"Flitting around to Van's subsidiaries in Dallas and San
Francisco and Mexico City. She always did flit. She was a
social butterfly, but now she's an iron one. She carries
clout. I imagine she'll be going to Mexico City for a
lengthy stay one of these days." He cocked his head at
her. "Why the sigh, little one? Are you tuckered out
already?" He looked at his watch. "At two o'clock on
Thanksgiving Day?"

Her sigh had been one of relief. This wasn't a man discussing his lover or even his girlfriend. No. Alex's mouth
was tilted with amusement. And he had called her, Erin
Kelly, "little one." Definitely a term of endearment.

"I'm not at all tuckered out." She smiled as she
crooked her arms behind her head for a good stretch, feeling the tension ease. "I'm just relaxing," When she
caught the teasing gleam in his eyes, she said, "All right,
Alex. There's more. What is it?"

"Cecile says," he recited, in a mocking tone of voice,
"that 'Daddy is flying off to New York for his holiday
without Erin Kelly. He's changed his mind about marrying
her and he has a new woman friend already.' "

"Cecile van Rijn," snapped Erin, "has a mouth that's
entirely too big. She blabs everything to everyone." But
Erin couldn't stay angry for more than a few seconds. She
started to laugh.

Alex joined in and soon they were both laughing, Alex
slapping his knee and Erin wiping her eyes. Darling Cecile.
If she had walked in the door that instant, Erin would have
hugged her.

"Kelly, I was taken in by that chick. I'm not sure how
or why, but I get the feeling I missed the boat somewhere.
There was a hell of a mixup."

Erin had torn open the candy wrapper during this latest admission and was starting to nibble a square of chocolate. She suddenly remembered her manners.

"Here, take this before I eat it all." She gave half the bar to Alex, then said gently, "It's really no wonder you were confused. If Van believed his own fairy tale, naturally Cecile believed it. Why shouldn't you?"

"Because I should have trusted my own instincts about you. After all, anyone driving a Saab can't be all bad." He reached over and gently tugged a lock of her hair. "And you did try to tell me."

Since it seemed the time for confessions, Erin said, "I admit, though, that I expected her to snap you up this summer."

"Snap me up? That spoiled kid?" Alex was astonished. "What gave you that idea? And just what do you mean by 'snap me up'?"

It was amazing. Alex was completely sincere, unaware of Cecile's plans for him, and had no idea how attractive he was to women. A wonderfully endearing trait.

"I meant either marriage or an affair." Erin smiled at him sweetly. "She gave me one progress report, and Step Two of your entrapment had just been accomplished when she decided I was a threat and stopped confiding in me."

"Progress report?" He was incredulous.

"You don't deny you took her out?"

"Hell, no. But, then, I've dated a lot of women."

"Not me."

He'd asked her out only that one time, never again, and the hurt popped out before she knew it was there. Miserable, Erin couldn't hide the hurt in her eyes, either.

"Hey." He reached over and gently tilted her chin so she had to look into his face.

"Never mind. It's over and done with," she said.

"Kelly . . ."

His eyes were blazing with feeling; dark, molten eyes whose small golden flecks emitted a tawny iridescence. Erin suddenly felt them warming her in a way the fire never could.

He moved closer, still facing her, until their knees were touching, then Alex took her hands in his.

"Listen to me, Erin Kelly."

"I'm listening," she said, but she looked out the window at the driving rain.

"*Erin.*" The commanding tone was so unmistakable that she quickly gave him her full attention. "I've taken out a lot of women," he said gruffly, "but that's only half the story."

He was holding her hands captive and, without realizing it, was holding them so tightly he was hurting her.

"I only take out women I don't care about," were the strange, husky words she heard. "For a long time I haven't wanted to care for anyone or get too close. Not until I met you."

She couldn't speak. Big-eyed, bewildered by his sudden unusual mood, Erin could only gape at him foolishly, not understanding.

"Come here."

She did as he said, wondering what memories made his face so drawn and hard, his mask in place once more. She crawled over and sat close beside him, wanting to comfort him, yet her soft body had begun to burn with desire as his long thigh and hard hip touched her.

"There, that's better." His arm went around her waist, and when Erin turned her face toward his, his mouth was waiting.

His lips moved softly over her own, the tip of his tongue teasing ever so gently. His hands, too, were gentle as they wandered over her cheeks and her softly rounded chin, exploring her ears and the delicate column of her throat.

How inexpressibly sweet it was, she thought, being so close to him, with the fire warming them and the rain outside. She offered up her gratitude on this Thanksgiving Day and followed it with a prayer: that this would truly be a new beginning for them, in all ways.

Alex, she now realized, had been hurt badly. He had been hurt possibly more than she, and Erin didn't know how she fit into the picture. It was horribly confusing. He cared for her—that much was obvious—but she needed more than that.

When he gave her a quick kiss on the mouth, followed by a teasing nip on the earlobe, she was relieved that his mood had changed. He drew her up by both hands and led her to a window, where they surveyed the dripping woods.

"This is the first good rain since spring. Let's just hope it goes easy."

She knew what he meant. The earth was rock hard and all but impermeable; almost all the water would run off.

"Come on. Let me show off some more new stuff."

The flagstones in the entry hall had been sealed and polished since she was last there and did, indeed, look like the bedrock of Otter Run, gleaming like wet rock, just as Alex had promised. She followed him about, from the basement, where she admired a small, neat furnace and shining copper pipes, to the second floor, where she praised the newly finished bathroom, complete with sauna and Jacuzzi.

She looked at Alex disconsolately. "I don't think Van will ever come here now."

"No," he agreed quietly, "and I know it will be hard for you to let it go."

She nodded, seeing nothing for the moment and feeling only emptiness. It would be almost as bad as losing a child whom one had watched grow to a strong and beautiful maturity.

She pushed the thought away. There was too much happiness this day to brood over Whitewater and what would become of it.

"What else is there?"

"The closets are finished in the master bedroom. His and hers." He grinned. "I think you'll like them."

She did. They were spacious and had cedar-lined compartments that smelled wonderful. She had just noticed a foam mattress and blankets in one corner of the room when Alex suddenly moved to the large windows that looked out over Otter Run.

"Alex, what *is* it?"

Erin rushed to his side and what she saw chilled her. The gentle creek had turned into a monster: muddy, churning, and frothing as logs and branches were carried along by the swift current.

They hurried to the opposite window, the one that looked out directly onto the falls, and saw the debris being hurled over them before rapidly disappearing downstream.

"Oh, *Alex.*"

She was frightened for the house, and his grim expression didn't relieve her concern.

"I heard there was to be wild weather up north. It's one reason I came up today."

"What can we do?" she wailed, putting both hands to her face.

"Not a damn thing. Pray, maybe."

She did. "Oh, dear Lord, guard this house," she murmured aloud. "*Please* watch over this house."

It was what Alex in his greater wisdom had warned her about all along: the stream. Chuckling, singing little Otter Run had turned wild, and could damage the foundation. She wrung her hands. Maybe this was the day he could say "I told you so."

"We may as well relax," Alex said. "Come back to the den."

The den was the right place to be with its bright, crackling fire. It was comforting. They put on more wood, sat on the warm hearth, and watched the rain as the wind began to rise, driving it horizontally.

Whitewater's broad windows, meant to bring the outdoors inside, did just that. It was as though they were in a nest in the bare trees, yet were securely anchored to earth. Safe in a quiet sanctuary from which they could watch the awesome power of nature.

Black clouds bursting with rain chased one another closely as they crowded into the small valley, and the wind . . . Erin shuddered as the wind wailed, searching all the corners of Whitewater to get in and, failing that, roared downstream to the lake, where it churned up whitecaps in its fury at being thwarted.

"I've never *seen* such a storm before," Erin said in a quavering voice as they heard the nearby rumble of thunder.

"We're safe, and the house is safe. Solid as Gibraltar. Don't worry." Alex's voice was reassuring, but his dark eyes, resting on the flames, were hooded and distant. His jaw was clamped tightly until his next words. "Erin, I want to tell you something."

"Of course." Here it comes, she thought, and sighed. The "I told you so." He was going to complain about Whitewater's being so close to the water. She pulled her bent knees against her chest, rested her chin on them, and waited, resigned.

"I've wanted to tell you about Francesca several times." He reached for her hand and held it between his own.

"Francesca?" Erin stiffened. "What a . . . pretty

name." Instantly she was jealous of the woman, whoever she was.

"She would have been my wife," said Alex, so low Erin almost didn't hear the words.

When his eyes met hers, she saw the emptiness in them again, the sadness she'd noticed before. It seemed such an alien thing in a man like Alex Butler.

Suddenly, instead of jealousy, Erin felt a keen resentment that this Francesca had hurt him so. Erin had never seen him this way, ashen, tears making his eyes shimmer.

"She was small and strong," he said softly. "Independent. Cocky. God, did she stand up to me." He pulled in and released a great breath. "She was like a pixie. An adorable pixie. Francesca was a lot like you . . ."

Erin, afraid to move, held her breath for a moment. This wasn't at all what she had expected. This had been a nightmare for Alex, a tragedy that now made the tears stream unashamed down his face.

"I was in Switzerland on a skiing vacation and I met her the day I arrived in Zermatt. For two weeks we skied and . . ." He hesitated.

Erin knew he had been about to say "made love," and she knew it was in deference to her, distraught as he was, that he continued with ". . . enjoyed each other's company."

Strangely, she didn't mind the thought of Alex and that unknown woman in each other's arms. No matter what had happened afterward, Erin could see that Francesca had made him truly happy then.

Alex's face was suddenly as wild and dark as the storm beyond the windows, and Erin shivered. His mood had changed. She wasn't sure what it was he wanted to crush and destroy with his bare hands. She knew only that his rage had to be released or he wouldn't have any peace the remainder of this day. Or maybe forever.

"My last days in Zermatt," he continued relentlessly, "we decided she would return to her home in Italy, then come to America as soon as she could."

Erin had seen that small muscle moving deep in his jaw before, had seen that anger in his eyes. Smoldering fury. What had Francesca done to him? It looked as though he would kill her if he ever laid hands on her again.

"Our last day there I wanted us just to . . . be together. Quietly. But Francesca loved to ski, so I gave in."

Erin knew instinctively what he was going to say next. She dreaded hearing it but knew he needed to tell her. She wondered, in fact, if he had told another soul, or had he held it inside himself, festering all this time?

When they came, the words were worse than she had feared. A crevasse, Alex continued, one that hadn't been there the day before, was suddenly beneath them and they'd both fallen in, Francesca first. He'd tried to check his descent but couldn't.

Erin's imagination supplied the rest. The girl's small figure disappearing into a horrifying, icy darkness; Alex hearing his beloved's screams as he himself crashed in after her.

"Oh, Alex. My *God*."

"She suffocated." The words were so low, she nearly missed them.

For a long time he didn't speak. The only sounds were the fire and the wind and Erin's soft weeping.

"I've tried to tell myself I couldn't have saved her even if I had been conscious. My leg was broken in three places."

"Oh, Alex."

He shook his head, sharply brushing off her sympathy, then apologized for his abruptness. "Sorry, I don't handle sympathy well."

"When did it happen?" Erin was almost afraid to speak.

"Five years ago."

He gently cradled her cheek and her chin, brushing her soft skin with his fingertips. "You're so like her, Erin. So small and sassy and beautiful. So fearless."

She shook her head sadly. "No, Alex. Francesca was fearless. I'm not. I'd be afraid to go hurtling down a mountain the way she did and I—"

It was then that the sound of the wind changed key, turning to a high keening, a wail that made them run to the window.

Otter Run was out of its bed.

Alex, followed closely by Erin, rushed to the living room and out onto the terrace. They peered over the parapet at the writhing, muddy water lapping the foundation and heard the thumping of wood against wood. With each thump, the terrace shuddered beneath their feet.

A large log was ramming into one supporting timber after another as it was whirled about in the frothing water. With every heavy buffet, Erin cringed, but it was Alex's strained face that caused the terror in her heart.

The vertical supports, intended to give Whitewater security during the coming snows, could now damage the house. The timbers, if they took a continual heavy barrage of debris, could seriously weaken the cantilevers.

Alex sprinted back into the house.

"Kelly, come on." She raced after him, first to the den, where they threw on their coats, then to the double garage, where he snatched up two sledgehammers. "*Here.*" He thrust one of them at her.

"What's happening?" she cried, stumbling after him, half falling because of the mud and the awkward weight of the sledgehammer.

"We've got to knock down the timbers," he shouted

above the wind, and waded into the swirling, knee-deep water.

"Alex, look out for the log!"

He swung his hammer at it, angrily swatting it out of his path, then he began throwing all his weight into knocking down the supports. One by one he plowed into them, with a fierce, white-hot fury that sent them crashing and splashing into the water, then spinning down toward the lake.

Erin strove to imitate Alex, holding the long handle with both hands and putting her back into swinging the hammer in a wide arc against the timbers. She felt a mother's fierceness as she defended her child from danger, a source of more strength than she knew she had. Her struggles netted her several timbers to Alex's dozen.

As Erin fought doggedly beside him, both oblivious of the biting wind, cold rain, and the freezing water swirling around them, she was fully aware of one thing: Alex's berserk fury was just what was needed for his healing to begin.

Chapter Twelve

❧

It was a flash flood, and the waters of Otter Run receded into their narrow, rocky bed almost as quickly as they had risen. Maybe they needn't have knocked down the supports, Erin thought after they had fearfully made an inspection of the outer perimeter of the house and found it sound. But, then, they hadn't known the storm would end so soon, and even sporadic battering over several hours might have caused structural cracking.

"She's okay," Alex said, but Erin was shocked by his haggard appearance, and she saw he was limping badly.

"We'd better get back inside," she said quietly.

He needed to get his leg warm, she thought, then remembered with terrible clarity why he limped. Everything had been pushed from her mind this past half hour save for the danger to Whitewater and the struggle to save it.

Now the crevasse loomed black and deep and hideous in her mind's eye. Erin knew she would have nightmares about it. A shudder swept her from head to toe, and for the first time she was aware of the wet, icy slacks plastered to her legs, the mud squishing in her shoes with every step, and her wet coat and hair.

Alex put a long arm around her waist, propelling her quickly toward the house.

"Your hands and face are almost blue with the cold,"

he said gruffly. "You're going to take a hot shower, and so am I—right after we check the basement."

She was almost afraid to look at the basement but, miraculously, they found it bone dry. Not even a trickle. Alex's insistence on three-foot-thick walls and her placing the door on a higher level had saved it.

He led her upstairs to the kitchen, where they left their muddy shoes and socks and their soaked coats. As she followed him toward the master bedroom and its luxurious bath, she realized her predicament for the first time.

"Alex, what am I going to wear? And you, too."

"I go through a lot of clothes up here, I always keep extras."

When they entered the bedroom, she saw the small, neat stack of clothing near the mattress. He chose a pair of faded jeans and a plaid flannel shirt, and put them in her hands.

"Here you go. There are clean towels in the bathroom."

He was avoiding her eyes, and the haunted shadow on his face and his drawn eyebrows twisted her heart. He was still shaken over his fear for the house, but now she knew what the other cause was, too. He was painfully vulnerable, much more so than she. At least she'd had happiness before losing it, but Alex's was gone before it could begin. Except for those two weeks . . .

She wanted to comfort him, to cover his face and body with her kisses, to try to make him happy again. How foolish they were, suffering alone when each could help the other.

"You think you can work that newfangled shower?" he asked, his voice still gruff. She nodded. "Good. I can scrounge up some more food for our Thanksgiving dinner. I have some canned stuff."

"Actually, I brought a pumpkin pie." She smiled up at him. "Homemade."

His eyes met hers then and Erin wondered what he saw in them to make him stop in his tracks and gaze down at her, almost startled. She knew how she felt inside: soft and warm, wanting him more than she could have believed possible, loving him beyond all reason. Maybe, she thought with a tremble, maybe it showed on her face.

"Erin?"

"Oh, Alex . . ."

He took a tentative step toward her and she went to him, shyly slipping her arms around his waist. She gently pressed him to her, laying her head on his hard chest as her hands stroked and patted his back in the age-old way of women. Protecting and comforting him.

"Alex, I love you," she whisperd. She was opening herself to him in every way, and when she looked up at him, at his face so far above her own, she saw wonder there. He kissed her lips then, such a joyous, hungry kiss that her heart seemed to brim over with the love she felt for him.

"Erin." He cradled her in his arms, nearly smothering her against him for the longest time. "I thought this would never happen again. I promised myself it wouldn't."

"Let what happen?" she gasped as he placed small, sweet kisses all over her face. She wanted to hear him say it, *needed* to hear him say it.

"My spunky little Kelly"—his hands were moving over her—"how you wielded that sledgehammer, and you said you weren't fearless. I love you. Dear God, how I love you."

She was trembling from head to foot, almost afraid to believe what she had heard.

"You're drenched and frozen. Come on. Into the shower with you." He pulled her into the spacious bathroom and flipped a switch. It was as though he had turned on the summer sun.

"Let's get you out of those clothes."

She was still shivering and chattering, even with the radiant warmth bathing her, and, to her delight, Alex took complete charge.

He turned on the shower, tugged off her sweater, and unhooked her bra, all very efficiently and businesslike. He then squatted and got down to work at peeling off the wet slacks that clung so stubbornly to her legs. When he finally pulled off her flimsy panties and tossed them to the floor, he grinned wolfishly.

"Kelly, you've got the sauciest little white rump." He gave her a gentle swat and then she felt his teeth, just as gently, nipping her buttocks. "Plump and firm and . . . hurry up. Get in there."

She laughed with delight and stepped from the column of desert sunlight into the steamy, tropical downpour of the shower. It was heaven, pure heaven. Her shivering ceased and her tension soon flowed away. Why not? Alex loved her and Whitewater was safe. Their house had weathered a terrible ordeal.

Eyes closed, water streaming down over her face, Erin soaped her hair and rinsed it until it squeaked. She was humming a silly little tune, humming with the pure joy of the moment, when two long arms went around her from behind. She squealed as Alex's hands closed over each of her breasts; dark against white, the black hair on his tanned arms an exciting contrast to her smooth skin.

He pulled her back against him, her buttocks squeezing against his excited hardness as his hands slid over her and he planted a smacking kiss on the back of her neck.

"Alex." She sagged against him. "You're making my legs wobble." She was weakened by his strength, weakened by his big, dark hands slipping over her soft flesh.

"Turn around." His husky voice was in her ear.

"Alex . . ." She was giggling, silly with excitement

and high spirits. "I'll fall down if you let me go, I swear I
will. Don't let go."

He turned her around, tilted her streaming, radiant
face, and gave her a deep kiss. "Kelly, I'll never let you
go."

Fire flamed deep inside as Alex pressed her to him and
the erect buds of her breasts met his chest. She felt his
hands, slippery with soap, smoothing slowly over her wet
body, following the curves and contours of her shoulders,
following the gentle indentation of her back before it
swelled into her rounded buttocks, and then slipping down
over her thighs.

"*Alex.* That tickles."

His lips tenderly brushed her small, gleaming head and
her slicked-back hair, then he found her mouth once more,
drinking in its sweetness along with the gentle spray that
enfolded their bodies in mist.

His hands took hers and placed the soap in them. "It's
your turn."

As he continued to stroke her satiny skin, skin so soft
and smooth that it offered no resistance to his caresses,
she shyly applied the soap to the mat of tough, springy
black curls on his chest.

"I've never done this before," she gasped, realizing for
the first time just how much she had missed.

"Then it's time you learned, lady."

Alex didn't need reflected candlelight for his eyes to
burn. They scanned her hungrily as her hands moved sensuously over his wide, hard-muscled shoulders, up his throat,
and over the rough skin of his unshaven face.

Her heart fluttered as he guided her hands down over the
rock-hard muscles of his stomach toward his tanned
thighs.

He pulled her so close then that even the water coursing
between their bodies was stopped and streamed elsewhere,

and she felt his hardness between her legs. When she squeezed them together, he sighed with pleasure.

"It's nearly time, little one."

He turned off the water, took one of his big towels, and tightly wrapped it around her so that her arms were imprisoned beneath it.

"What a sweet little bundle I've got." He laughed huskily and moved his hands over her body in a circular pattern to dry her.

Her breathing was irregular. In fact, it sometimes seemed as though she forgot to breathe at all.

Alex dried himself quickly, then she was lifted high in his arms and he proudly showed her their reflection in the full-length mirror at the far end of the bath by the Jacuzzi.

Her breath caught in her throat. She had never looked more radiant: her cheeks pink and her eyes gleaming like azure gems beneath her still-damp cap of auburn hair, and her body had never looked so luscious—white as cream with her breasts full, peaked, pink-tipped, standing up for his hungry mouth to taste them.

And Alex, with his powerful, long legs apart, was a dark Atlas bearing his burden so easily, his lean arms wrapped tightly about her, his black hair tousled, his eyes hot with hunger and anticipation.

"Oh, Alex, I love you so much, I—" When his mouth stopped her words, Erin's arms went around his neck. Within seconds, she was being lowered to the mattress in the corner of the bedroom.

His eyes glittered over her and a little shiver brushed her skin. She was as eager for lovemaking as Alex, but now that she was in his bed, she knew she would stay there until he released her, until he was completely satisfied. The thought both titillated and unnerved her. He could be so gentle, yet that primitive look on his face was just a bit frightening . . .

He nuzzled her breast, his voice low and thick with passion. "If anyone had told me this morning that I'd have such a delectable woman in my bed today, I'd have thought he was crazy."

Erin's breath came in soft shudders as he did what he would with her; his hands stroking her and his mouth and tongue tasting and teasing, searching out the most exquisitely sensitive parts of her body. She was helpless. Even the sight of his dark body, the long, dark, powerful length of him beside her, left her without strength.

"Alex, I—I'm sorry. I seem to be weak as a kitten," she whispered. "You affect me in the strangest way."

"Weak as a kitten, hmm?" He swept a devilish glance over her. That's just the way I want you for now, little one. Soft and weak and adorable. You can be a tigress another time."

He cupped a breast in each hand, sharply peaking them, taking each tip between his teeth to inflict an excruciatingly sweet, small pain before encircling the wider pinkness with his tongue. It was an ecstatic, maddening sensation that made her arch involuntarily against him, made her feel open and hot and pulsing.

His arm slipped beneath her then, and he pulled her close so that they lay on their sides, their bodies pressed together full length, from their lips to the tips of their toes. His knee thrust between her legs, forcing them apart, and his hand was suddenly there, shocking her, his seeking fingers parting the entrance to the very center of her sensual arousal. It was as though fire and ice were touching her. Her pleasure was near its peak when he ceased himself into her and they were united.

"*Alex.*" She could only gasp his name before his mouth took hers again, silencing her.

There was little time left for either of them, but what there was seemed enchanted. She knew with every part of her that outside it was still raining, but peacefully now, and she could hear the torrent of the stream, wild still, but not threatening.

Almost forgetting to breathe, Erin finally gave herself up to the sweet blackness. A blackness into which she was spun crazily and in which she clung to Alex fiercely, crying out her delight. A blackness in which her ecstasy was many things: the warm, dark openness of her mouth and her body, so soft and thirsting for him, the hardness and the hungry thrusting within her, and the sweet knowledge that this man possessing her was *her* man. And there was the torrent. The torrent that had always been there, sometimes a torrent of electricity or of excitement or fire; but now it was a torrent of love that joined them, every bit as wild and deep and dangerous as the torrent that roared beneath them.

Afterward they lay in each other's arms for what seemed an endless time, their lips and bodies sealed. When she moved in his arms, in a half slumber, it was as though Alex couldn't, wouldn't, give her up. As though if she left his arms, he would never find her again.

And then she would feel his body and his tongue stirring her again: gentle movements, small at first, then rapidly growing and claiming her. Primitive, lusty lovemaking that left her drained but hungry for more. Finally, when they were both satisfied, they went to the Jacuzzi only to make love again. Gently this time.

Alex dried her as he had earlier, then carried her to the foam mattress. He tenderly tucked her in, crawled under the cover beside her, and sighed. A long sigh that was both contented and exhausted.

"Kelly, I love you," he murmured, and promptly fell asleep.

Erin turned on her side and looked at him, a smile curving her lips. Who would have thought what her

Thanksgiving Day would hold? Alex Butler. A man she had loved these past months but a man from whom she never expected to hear such words as "Kelly, I love you."

She murmured his name as he slept and moved her hands lightly over his body, outlining its perfect contours. Everything about him was strong and beautiful, indestructible—and the very symbol of this house she loved. And he loved her. Erin kept returning to that same wondrous thought again and again.

She contemplated him tenderly: the silken lashes resting on his cheeks, sooty hair curving every which way over his well-shaped head, his dark hand lying on his chest.

Life with him would never be dull, she mused. She would gladly serve as his co-driver in rallies, unless, of course, she decided to compete with him. She was tickled by the thought. Saab against Saab. When he flew, however, she would only be a passenger.

Very gently Erin smoothed Alex's tousled hair and kissed his fingers. She mustn't forget the peace and support he was able to give her in such large measure. Yes, his body would be both a haven and a source of excitement, like Whitewater. Their love was fully grown now, after all these months of trial and uncertainty, fully grown and strong—able to withstand any stress or storms that came its way. Again, like Whitewater.

She sat up suddenly. She'd been so happy today that she had managed to forget reality, the reality of what would surely happen to Whitewater. Van and Cecile would never come here, and the place would be sold—this house that she and Alex had built and defended. And now they had made love here, joining them to it even more closely.

Alex woke and put his arm around her waist, pulling her down beside him.

"Erin, what's wrong? Ah, don't tell me." He grinned and nuzzled her shoulder. "You want more."

"Oh, I can manage to wait." She threw him an impish look. —

"For a woman who'll soon be married, you don't look too happy. Hell, I thought you'd be ecstatic at having 'snapped me up.' "

"Married? I haven't agreed to that, Alexander Butler. You haven't asked me, for one thing."

Before she could say another word, Erin was imprisoned in his arms, and his eyes were serious. "Kelly, no joking on this subject. Ever."

It was almost shocking, she thought gravely. He was so big and strong and yet so vulnerable.

"Will you marry me?" he asked quietly.

"Just try to get away." She snuggled as close to him as possible and sniffed his warm, bare skin. How she loved him, the feel and the smell of him—everything about him.

"Then why the misery, little one? What is it?"

"You know how Van is." She spooned herself against him, positioning his hands so that they held her breasts. "He's so keen on getting a return on his investments that I'm terrified he'll sell this place. And if that happens . . ." She shook her head, unable to bear the thought. "It makes me sick to think about it."

She felt his lips brushing her hair. "Kelly, I've been meaning to tell you. The house was sold. Yesterday."

She stiffened. "Sold? Who *bought* it, Alex? Oh, Lord, don't tell me. I don't want to know—I hate them already."

"You hate them, huh?" Alex growled. He turned her around to face him, intent on kissing the velvety hollow of her throat.

"Alex, I'm sorry. I'm in no mood. I'm far too upset . . ." She tried to push him away, but it was too late. His mouth was locked on the dusky-rose, puckered center of one breast, and his arms and legs were wrapped about her, holding her fast.

She was already hot inside, and the familiar, tantalizing sensuous currents were flowing between them again, burning, demanding, ready to draw them together in another breathless spin on their own private torrent of love.

He lifted his lips from her swollen breast. "Kelly, you don't act as though you hate me."

Her eyes widened and there was time only for her to murmur, "*You*," before she was lost in the deep sweetness of Alex's kiss.

It was nearly dusk when they awakened to snow; big soft flakes drifting down, as pure and sweet as a benediction. A blessing on Whitewater.

Erin dressed warmly in Alex's rolled-up jeans, a blue-and-white plaid flannel shirt, and a pair of his very large wool socks. She padded about, using a hot plate to heat the contents of the cans Alex had opened, turkey stew and sweet potatoes. She put out paper plates and plastic forks, then made the coffee. Dessert would be the pumpkin custard pie.

They ate by the den fire, talking excitedly all the while, for Alex had saved his big news for dinner. Yesterday, he said, Cecile had revealed that the house and the land, all seven hundred acres of it, were to go on the market.

Erin listened, wide-eyed, as Alex described his phone call to Van in New York. He had made an offer Van couldn't refuse, and they had made a gentleman's agreement. The documents would be drawn up and signed on Van's return.

Alex fortified himself with several pieces of pie before they moved to a window and stood looking out at the last few moments of daylight.

"Whitewater's first snowfall," he said, putting his arms around her.

Erin leaned her head against his chest. She could still make out the lacy flakes falling softly, outlining branches and rocks and enfolding Whitewater in a peaceful blanket.

"And to think Whitewater is yours." It was still hard to believe any of the day's events.

"Ours," he answered firmly.

"Ours, then . . ."

In her mind's eye, Erin suddenly saw two children flitting among the dark trees across the creek. They were shadowy and faceless, of an indeterminate age, but both had Alex's sooty, silken hair. She loved the very thought of them.

A small panic leaped to her throat. Whitewater was such a perfect place for children, but how could she assume Alex would want any? Carl hadn't, and Alex, too, was a busy, important man, on his way up.

His arms tightened around her. "Kelly, can't you just picture our kids over there in the woods throwing snowballs?"

He'd done it again, had read her thoughts, and it was as though the sun had just sailed out from behind a black cloud.

"Oh, Alex, I can. I can see them now." She was warmed by relief and by her growing love for this man whose strong arms held her. "I *love* you," she said again. When she lifted her face for his kiss, it seemed like a seal, a pledge between them.

"On this one day," she said, "I've gotten everything I've ever wanted, and all from you."

He smiled. "You're not so bad at giving either, little one."

Alex turned her around so that she faced him, then took

her in his arms as his mouth covered hers in a very tender, gentle kiss.

She knew what he wanted and she was willing to give— and give and give. But he was carrying her to the kitchen, not the bedroom, and he stood her on her feet.

"How about giving me some more of that pie now? And more coffee."

Seeing the surprised look on her face, he chuckled and added, "That, too, Kelly. That, too. But there's all of tonight, and all of tomorrow."

Erin nodded and cut a piece of pie. "And all of forever."

TELL US YOUR OPINIONS AND RECEIVE A FREE COPY
OF THE RAPTURE NEWSLETTER.

Thank you for filling out our questionnaire. Your response to the following questions will help us to bring you more and better books. In appreciation of your help we will send you a free copy of the Rapture Newsletter.

1. Book Title:_____

   Book # :_____ (5-7)

2. Using the scale below how would you rate this book on the following features? Please write in one rating from 0–10 for each feature in the spaces provided. Ignore bracketed numbers.

(Poor) 0 1 2 3 4 5 6 7 8 9 10 (Excellent)
                                        0–10 Rating

Overall Opinion of Book. . . . . _____ (8)
Plot/Story. . . . . _____ (9)
Setting/Location. _____ (10)
Writing Style. . . . . _____ (11)
Dialogue. . . . . _____ (12)
Love Scenes. . . . . _____ (13)
Character Development:
Heroine:. . . . . _____ (14)
Hero:. . . . . _____ (15)
Romantic Scene on Front Cover. . . . . _____ (16)
Back Cover Story Outline . . . . _____ (17)
First Page Excerpts. . . . . _____ (18)

3. What is your: Education: Age:_____ (20-22)

      High School (   )1   4 Yrs. College (   )3
      2 Yrs. College (   )2   Post Grad   (   )4 (23)

4. Print Name:_____

   Address:_____

   City:_____State:_____Zip:_____

   Phone # (   )_____ (25)

Thank you for your time and effort. Please send to New American Library, Rapture Romance Research Department, 1633 Broadway, New York, NY 10019.

RAPTURE ROMANCE

*Provocative and sensual,
passionate and tender—
the magic and mystery of love
in all its many guises*

Coming next month

SEPTEMBER SONG by Lisa Moore. Swearing her career came first, Lauren Rose faced the challenge of her life in Mark Landrill's arms, for she had to choose between the work she thrived on—and a passion that left her both fulfilled and enslaved . . .

A MOUNTAIN MAN by Megan Ashe. For Kelly March, Josh Munroe's beloved mountain world was a haven where she could prove her independence. but Josh—who tormented her with desire—resented the intrusion. Could Kelly prove she was worth his love—and, if she did, would she lose all she'd fought to achieve?

THE KNAVE OF HEARTS by Estelle Edwards. Brilliant young lawyer Kate Sewell had no defense against carefree riverboat gambler Hal Lewis. But could Kate risk her career—even for the ecstasy his love promised?

BEYOND ALL STARS by Melinda McKenzie. For astronaut Ann Lafton, working with Commander Ed Saber brought emotional chaos that jeopardized their NASA shuttle mission. But Ann couldn't stop dreaming that this sensuous lover would fly her to the stars . . .

DREAMLOVER by JoAnn Robb. Painter K.L. Michaels needed Hunter St. James to pull off a daring masquerade, but she didn't count on losing her relaxed lifestyle as their wild love affair unfolded. Could their nights of sensual fireworks make up for their daily battles?

A LOVE SO FRESH by Marilyn Davids. Loving Ben Heron was everything Anna Markham needed. But she considered marriage a trap, and Ben, too, had been burned before. Passion drew them together, but was their rapture enough to overcome the obstacles they faced?

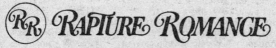

RAPTURE ROMANCE

Provocative and sensual, passionate and tender— the magic and mystery of love in all its many guises

New Titles Available Now

To order, use coupon on the next page.

RAPTURE ROMANCE

*Provocative and sensual,
passionate and tender—
the magic and mystery of love
in all its many guises*

**Buy them at your local
bookstore or use coupon
on next page for ordering.**

RAPTURE ROMANCE

Provocative and sensual, passionate and tender— the magic and mystery of love in all its many guises

SPECIAL $1.00 REBATE OFFER
WHEN YOU BUY
FOUR RAPTURE ROMANCES

To receive your cash refund, send:

1. This coupon: To qualify for the $1.00 refund, this coupon, completed with your name and address, must be used. (Certificate may not be reproduced)

2. Proof of purchase: Print, on the reverse side of this coupon, the *title* of the books, the *numbers* of the books (on the upper right hand of the front cover preceding the price), and the U.P.C. numbers (on the back covers) on your next four purchases.

3. Cash register receipts, with prices circled to:
   Rapture Romance $1.00 Refund Offer
   P.O. Box NB037
   El Paso, Texas 79977

Offer good only in the U.S. and Canada. Limit one refund/response per household for any group of four Rapture Romance titles. Void where prohibited, taxed or restricted. Allow 6–8 weeks for delivery. Offer expires March 31, 1984.

NAME_____

ADDRESS_____

CITY_____STATE_____ZIP_____

SPECIAL $1.00 REBATE OFFER
WHEN YOU BUY
FOUR RAPTURE ROMANCES

See complete details on reverse

1. Book Title _____

Book Number 451-_____

U.P.C. Number 7116200195-_____

2. Book Title _____

Book Number 451-_____

U.P.C. Number 7116200195-_____

3. Book Title _____

Book Number 451-_____

U.P.C. Number 7116200195-_____

4. Book Title _____

Book Number 451-_____

U.P.C. Number 7116200195-_____

U.P.C. Number

0   SAMPLE

71162 00195